Could things get any worse?

"Is that all you can talk about? Utah?" I shouted at my father, my hands balling into fists. "I guess you're going to tell us how great and fabulous and perfect living there is going to be, right? Well, you know what? I think it's going to be the worst thing that ever happened to me."

"Jessica—"

"Oh, wait!" I said, ignoring my dad's stern tone. "The worst thing that ever happened to me already happened. This afternoon. Damon and I broke up. Wanna know why?" I said, glaring at my father. "Because of you! Damon hates me, and it's all your fault! You don't care about anybody!"

I turned, ran out of the dining room, and took the stairs two at a time. I slammed the door to my room and turned the lock, even though I was strictly forbidden to ever lock my door. I didn't care about my parents' stupid rules anymore. I didn't care about anything they had to say.

Don't miss any of the books in SWEET VALLEY JUNIOR HIGH, an exciting series from Bantam Books!

Too Many
Good-byes

Written by
Jamie Suzanne

Created by
FRANCINE PASCAL

BANTAM BOOKS
NEW YORK · TORONTO · LONDON · SYDNEY · AUCKLAND

To Margaret Abigail Chardiet

RL 4, 008–012

TOO MANY GOOD-BYES
A Bantam Book / June 2001

Sweet Valley Junior High is a trademark of Francine Pascal.
Conceived by Francine Pascal.
Cover photography by Michael Segal.

Produced by 17th Street Productions,
an Alloy Online, Inc. company.
33 West 17th Street
New York, NY 10011.

ISBN: 0-553-48732-9

Visit us on the Web! www.randomhouse.com/kids

Published simultaneously in the United States and Canada

Bantam Books is an imprint of Random House Children's Books, a
division of Random House, Inc. BANTAM BOOKS and the rooster
colophon are registered trademarks of Random House, Inc. Bantam Books,
1540 Broadway, New York, New York 10036.

PRINTED IN THE UNITED STATES OF AMERICA

OPM   0 9 8 7 6 5 4 3 2 1

Elizabeth's Journal

I am so pathetic. Totally pathetic. I just spent about an hour sitting in my room, listening to my tape of slow songs and doodling in my notebook. That's pathetic enough, right? Well, guess what I was doodling?

Sal + Elizabeth

Elizabeth + Sal

In about a million different sizes and handwritings. Plus a bunch of hearts and stars and clouds and rainbows.

Oh, and a big drawing of Utah with a huge red X through it.

So yes, I'm a loser. But I'm also so . . . mad. All this time, Sal and I have been just friends, when all this time, we could have been together. And now it's too late. Now we're moving to Utah, which is hundreds of miles away, and I'll probably never see Sal again. And we'll never know. We'll never know if our best-friendship would have made us the perfect couple.

All I know is I'm going to miss him so much. It's not fair. It's just not fair.

Jessica's Journal

<u>Ten Ways to Break the News to Damon</u>

1. Send him an e-mail.
2. Write him a note and stick it in his locker.
3. Skywriting (look into cost).
4. Throw him a party and write <u>I'm moving!</u> across the top of the cake.
5. Have it read during morning announcements.
6. Leak the news to his little sisters. They'll definitely spill, and he can't kill them.
7. Take out an ad in <u>Zone</u>.
8. Tell Lacey. It'll take her two seconds to "innocently slip" in front of Damon.
9. Tell him I'm dying of some rare disease. Once he's done crying, tell him I was kidding—I'm just moving. Then he'll be so relieved, he'll even be happy!
10. Make Dad tell him. This is all his fault anyway.

Damon's Journal

For the last few days something hasn't felt right with Jessica. She's been acting all . . . out of it. Like, staring off into space while we're eating lunch and getting all quiet when we're around her friends. And believe me, Jessica is never quiet around her friends. She loves to talk.

Just not lately. Not even on the phone at night. For the past couple of months we've been talking on the phone every night before we go to bed. I know, it sounds dorky, but it wasn't like it was planned. It just started happening, and then it became such a regular part of my day that if I didn't call her, I felt like I was forgetting something. And those calls are always so great. Sometimes we talk about nothing, and sometimes we get into these great conversations about deep stuff. You know, like, life and stuff.

But the last few nights those phone calls haven't been the same. Sometimes she makes an excuse to get off the phone really quickly and sometimes . . .

Sometimes I think she's not even listening to me.

And that gets me wondering. What if she's going to break up with me?

Jessica

I woke up on Sunday morning and could barely pry my eyes open. They felt all puffy and were swollen shut. For a second I wondered if someone had given me a couple of black eyes in my sleep. When I rolled over and finally blinked them open, the sunlight streaming through my bedroom window stung my eyes. I was exhausted, and my nose was all stuffy. Maybe I was still dreaming. I couldn't be this tired after a whole night of sleep.

I rolled over onto my other side, putting my back to the window, and sighed. Something was definitely wrong, but in my half-asleep daze I couldn't remember what it was. Then I spotted my journal flung on the floor next to my bed along with a bunch of balled-up tissues, and it all came rushing back. I was moving to Utah. Well, not just me—my whole family.

My heart felt like it was collapsing in on itself, and a tear spilled across my cheek and onto my pillow. My father had made the announcement a few days ago—he was offered a new job in Utah, and we were all going to have to just stop our lives and follow him there. (He didn't say exactly that, but that was what he meant.) The last few days had been horrific for me and my sister, Elizabeth, and our brother, Steven. I hadn't even told any of my friends yet. I was kind of hoping something would happen—that my dad would take it all back and I'd never have to tell them anything. I hadn't even told my boyfriend, Damon.

I held my breath when I thought of him, fighting off another heart pang. That was why my journal was out. I'd spent half the night trying to come up with a way to break the news, but I still had no idea what to do. I felt like I would die in the process of telling him. I wouldn't be able to handle the look on his face. I'd just . . . die.

"Kids!" my father's voice boomed up the stairs. "Breakfast is ready!"

"Yeah, right," I muttered, pulling my purple comforter over my head and rolling over again so that my back now faced the door. I didn't want to have anything to do with my dad. I'd rather starve. He was taking me away from my home, my school, my friends, and the best boyfriend anyone could ever have, and I was just supposed to go down there and gobble up his blueberry pancakes like nothing was wrong? Whatever. I was never going to forgive him.

I heard the door to my bedroom open, and

my whole face went red with anger. I bunched up my sheet and gripped it in front of me. I knew it was my mother coming to tear me out of bed and make me go downstairs. Jessica, give your father a break, she would say. This is hard for him too. And you're only making it harder. Please! All Dad cared about was his stupid new job and all the money and prestige. If he cared about us, he would have at least asked us what we thought before deciding to ruin our lives.

"Jess?"

It was Elizabeth. I popped my head out from under the covers. "Close the door!" I whispered. She did—very quietly—and then sat down on the edge of my bed.

"Did you sleep?" she said.

"Kind of," I answered.

"I feel like I haven't had a real sleep in days," she said with a yawn. She was still wearing her white tank-top pajamas, and her hair was a mess. There was a knot the size of a baseball in the back, and I knew she was going to have some serious trouble getting it out. She leaned over, pulled down the blankets, and crawled into bed next to me, resting her head on my shoulder.

I sighed and almost smiled. No matter what happened, at least no one would ever take me away from Elizabeth.

Elizabeth

"I don't ever want to get up," Jessica said, her voice all flat and toneless.

"I know what you mean," I answered, yawning and closing my tired, dry eyes. "What's the point? Our lives are over." Jessica giggled, and I turned my head to look at her. "How can you laugh at a time like this?" I asked.

"Sorry," she answered. "That just sounded more like something I would say."

"Yeah," I said, a small smile sneaking onto my lips. "That's true."

"Remember when we switched places at the beginning of the year and I made you plan the homecoming dance?" Jessica said, sounding wistful.

I groaned. "Yeah. I remember that no one bought it for a second," I said, remembering how all of Jessica's friends had just played along to humor us. They'd seen right through my unconvincing Jessica act.

"It's so weird," Jessica said as she twirled a lock of golden blond hair around her finger. "We pulled that off at SVMS a million times, and no one ever suspected a thing."

Hmmm. I'd never thought about it that way before. "I guess our new friends knew us better than we thought they did," I said with a thoughtful frown. Anna and Salvador hadn't believed Jessica was me either. We were way too close for that.

"I can't believe I'm never going to see Sal and Anna again," I said, propping myself up on one elbow so I could look at Jessica. "Remember how freaked we were that we were going to have to make all new friends?"

"I know!" Jessica exclaimed. She brought her hands up to hide her face and sighed. "You're so lucky you already told them. I don't know what I'm going to do."

"You just have to do it," I told her. "Like pulling off a Band-Aid. Once it's out there, you won't have to worry about it anymore. The longer you wait, the worse it's going to be."

She pulled down her hands and fiddled with the hem of the comforter that was stretched across her stomach. "You're probably right. I just wish—"

"Girls?"

My mom walked into the room, cutting Jessica off. I immediately plopped back down onto my back, and Jessica and I both stared straight ahead as if she weren't even there. I know it's immature, but it felt like my parents were the enemy. All they wanted to do was try to make us feel better about the fact that they were totally messing up our lives.

"C'mon, girls," Mom said, one hand on the doorknob, the other on her hip. "It's a beautiful day. Are you just going to stay in here and mope?"

"That was the general plan," Jessica said.

My mom sat down on the edge of the bed, pinning my leg down with the sheet. I glanced at her face, and she was all smiles. Bright eyed and happy as if nothing at all was wrong.

"You two are going to have to snap out of this," she said, putting her hand on the comforter over my leg and squeezing my ankle. "It's not like this move is the end of the world. You'll still have each other, and I know you'll have no trouble making friends."

I rolled my eyes, and I knew Jessica did too. "You guys just don't get it," I said.

"What don't we get?" my mom asked, the happiness dying off a bit. She put her hands in her lap and laced her fingers together.

"What about Damon?" Jessica wailed, finally sitting up. "He's the greatest guy ever, and I'm just supposed to dump him? 'Sorry, Damon, but my parents need to live in the middle of nowhere!'" she said sarcastically.

My mom's eyes narrowed, which I should

have taken as a warning, but I needed to vent too. "And what about my friends?" I added. "I just . . . I mean Sal and I just . . . and if I leave now . . ." I couldn't complete a sentence because I hadn't told my mom that Salvador and I had kissed, and now didn't seem like the right moment. But she had to see how upset I was.

"And what about the track team?" Jessica interrupted.

"And *Zone*?" I added.

"And Bethel and Kristin . . ."

"And Anna and Blue . . ."

"All right! That's enough!" my mom said sternly, standing up.

My heart skipped a few beats, and Jessica and I glanced at each other, shocked. My mom hadn't shouted, but she'd definitely raised her voice. She almost never raised her voice. Not even when we'd tried to bake one big cookie out of one of those long tubes of dough and practically burned the house down.

"You two sound like you're four years old," she said, in a more normal tone. "You're so busy complaining, you've forgotten what's most important—you're still here."

I looked down at my lap as my eyes filled with tears. I hated this. All of it.

"And while you're still here, you should make

the most of it," she added. "We are all leaving friends behind . . . even your father," she said pointedly. "But instead of moping and acting like children, we should all enjoy the next few weeks. We're not moving tomorrow, remember."

Jessica sighed and started picking at her fingernails. It looked like she felt just as guilty as I did. "Sorry, Mom," she muttered quietly.

"Yeah, sorry," I added, not looking up.

"And girls," she said, "go easy on your dad. It's not easy for him, knowing this decision has made you all so miserable. You should try to be supportive."

"We will," I said.

"We will," Jessica echoed.

"Good. I knew I could count on you two," Mom said, leaning over and running her hands over our hair. We both looked up at her with forced smiles. "Now, come down for breakfast. Your father's been cooking up a storm."

"We'll be right down," I said.

She smiled and walked out, leaving the door open. She probably thought if she did that, we'd smell my dad's pancakes and stop feeling sorry for ourselves. But that wasn't about to happen.

Jessica and I took one look at each other, flopped back down on the bed, and pulled the covers up over our heads. We weren't done feeling sorry for ourselves yet.

Jessica

"I think I have a fever, Liz, I'm serious," I said on Monday morning as my sister and I slowly walked the last stretch of sidewalk before we were in view of the school. I grabbed her hand and put it against my forehead. "Don't you think I'm hot?" I asked, my eyes wide.

"Yeah, maybe because it's ninety degrees out," she answered, pulling her hand away.

She was right that it was an unusually hot day for this time of year—even for southern California. But it was gorgeous out. The sun was shining, there wasn't a cloud in the sky, and there was a little ocean-scented breeze keeping it from being too unbearable. Everyone would probably head right for the beach after school today. I realized with a start that soon there would be no afternoon beach breaks. There would be no beach—period.

I looked up at the school as we turned onto one of the paths that lead to the front door, and my heart started pounding.

"I can't do this, Liz!" I said, slowing even

12

more. Elizabeth and I had both decided at the end of last week that it was time to come clean to all our friends about moving to Utah. And that meant coming clean to Damon. Today. And that was the last thing on earth I wanted to do.

"Yes, you can," Elizabeth said, shooting me a reassuring look. "Just go up to him and spit it out. It's not like he's going to be mad at you or something. This isn't your fault."

"You're right, you're right, I know you're right," I said, nodding and staring at the school. "It's just that . . . I feel like if I tell him, it'll be true."

"Sorry to break it to you, Jess, but it's true whether you tell him or not," Elizabeth said, smoothing the front of her perfectly white T-shirt.

Leave it to Elizabeth to give the reality check. A few kids who were standing in a clump by the door moved inside, and then I saw Damon. My heart pounded harder just at the sight of him waiting for me. He was wearing beat-up, wrinkled chinos and a red T-shirt, and his hair was perfectly messy. He looked amazing.

"There he is," I said, swallowing hard. "Look at him, Liz. He's so sweet and innocent and perfect and cute. How am I going to leave him?"

"It's gonna be okay," Elizabeth said.

I couldn't see how.

Elizabeth said hello to Damon and then shot

me a firm look, as if she was telling me I could do it. Then she walked ahead.

"Hey, Jess," Damon said with a lopsided smile.

Suddenly I felt totally self-conscious. Like he could just look at me and see right through to my brain and know I was hiding something.

"Hi," I said, clutching my books to my chest with both arms. What was I supposed to say now? Normally I'd ask him how his weekend was and tell him about everything I'd done. In fact, normally I would have talked to him over the weekend and seen him too. But all I'd done was avoid him—and sit around, cry, sit around, sniffle, sit around some more. Damon was looking at me with a question in his eyes. I must've looked ridiculous standing there silently arguing with myself.

"So . . . wanna go inside?" he asked finally.

"Yeah," I answered.

Damon held the door open for me, and I slipped into the lobby. He's always doing polite stuff like that. Where was I ever going to find another ninth-grade guy who did polite stuff like that without even thinking about it?

I wanted to tell him how great he was. And how much I appreciated that he treated me like a friend and a human being instead of just some babe he was going out with. But I had this huge

Jessica

lump in my throat, and I knew if I started talking, I would start to cry.

Instead we just walked through the lobby in a
sort of awkward silence. I hadn't felt so uncomfortable around Damon in ages—since before I
knew he liked me. So much for making the
most of my time in Sweet Valley.

Damon

I shoved my hands in my pockets and tried not to look as totally confused as I was. Normally Jessica held my hand when we walked into school together. And normally she gave me a kiss on the cheek when she saw me waiting for her in front of school. Now she was acting like she didn't even want to be near me, let alone touch me. She hadn't even told me about her weekend, and she was walking like a robot—completely rigid.

Something was definitely up.

I took a deep breath and tried not to panic as we turned down the main hall. There had to be something I could say to make it all better. Something perfect to say to remind her of how much I liked her and keep her from breaking up with me. But I didn't know what was wrong, so I couldn't imagine what the perfect thing to say would be. What had I done?

"So . . . uh . . . how was your weekend?" I said finally.

16

"Um . . . okay," she said. Her voice came out a little squeaky. "I didn't do much."

"Oh . . . really?" I said. I was so lame.

"Yeah," she answered.

Somehow I could tell that was the end of the conversation. We were walking silently again, so I had time to think this over. Okay, if she hadn't done much, maybe that meant she wasn't feeling well. Yeah! That was it. Maybe she'd been sick over the weekend, and it had started a little last week, and that's why she'd been acting so weird. It had nothing to do with me.

I glanced at her out of the corner of my eye and realized she did look a little pale. She'd pulled her hair back in a ponytail, which she only did when she ran track and couldn't care less what it looked like. And she was kind of sweaty, actually. She was definitely sick. Cool.

Then I felt guilty for hoping my girlfriend was sick. What kind of jerk was I anyway? But at least a stomach flu or a cold would pass. Breaking up would be a lot more permanent. And if she ever broke up with me . . .

"Hey, Damon. Jess." Luckily Blue Spiccoli came up to us and stopped my pathetic train of thought right in its tracks.

"Hey, man," I said.

"Hi, Blue!" Jessica exclaimed, as if she'd never

been so happy to see anyone in her life. "What's going on?" I glanced at her, surprised. She was looking at Blue, all bright eyed. So she had enough energy to talk to him but couldn't say two words to me. What was up?

"Have you guys seen Liz?" Blue asked, running a hand through his blond hair, which just fell right back onto his forehead.

"Yeah, she's probably headed for her locker," Jessica said with a smile. "Want me to help you find her?" She moved toward him like she was about to grab his arm and take off. Blue backed up a step.

"No, that's okay," he said, eyeing her like he thought she might explode. So I wasn't the only one who'd noticed how weird she was acting. "I know where her locker is. Thanks."

"Later, man," I said as Blue took off. He held up his hand in a wave. I looked at Jessica, and she just smiled tightly, turned, and followed in the direction Blue was going—toward her locker as well.

I felt like I was about to be sick. Yep. She was definitely going to break up with me.

Blue

I wiped my hands on the front of my favorite blue-and-green board shorts and slowly headed for Elizabeth's locker. I wasn't totally sure why I was doing this. After all, I was still mad at her. She'd kissed Salvador. Just the thought of it made me clench my hands into fists. If anything, Elizabeth should be looking for me—begging me to forgive her. I'd liked her for so long, and then the second it finally seemed like something was going to come of it, she threw me over for Salvador. It was a bad scene.

I tried to push my anger aside as I rounded the corner into the hallway where Elizabeth's locker was. After all, I wanted to have a normal conversation with her. There was no reason to make a scene in front of the entire school. All I wanted her to do was say the whole thing with Salvador was a total mistake. I wanted her to pick me. That wouldn't be so hard, would it? If she did that, I could be the big man and get over the monster chip on my shoulder.

Blue

The second I spotted her, I froze. She was standing a little ways down the hall, wearing a white T-shirt and a light blue flowered skirt. Her hair was back in a braid, and man, she just looked so pretty. Before I could blink, she turned and looked me directly in the eye. For a split second she looked almost scared, but then she sort of half smiled. Maybe this wasn't a lost cause. Maybe she really would pick me, and we could at least hang out together until she moved. Whenever that was going to happen.

I rolled back my shoulders and started walking in her direction. But I'd barely taken a step when the door at the other end of the hallway opened and Salvador walked through. Salvador was still on crutches after hurting his leg at the dance, but he was laughing. Anna Wang was beside him, and it looked like she was carrying his books. She had a stack in her arms that was bigger than she was. But I wasn't really looking at her. All I could do was stare at Salvador—my former friend—and wish he'd disappear.

Elizabeth's eyebrows knit together, and she turned around to see what I was glaring at and spotted Salvador. When she turned back to look at me again, she had this . . . light in her eyes. This bright, sparkling light that made her even more beautiful. And she had a big smile on her face.

My heart had broken before, when Elizabeth had told me about kissing Salvador. But standing in that hall, seeing that smile . . . that hurt way worse than I could have even imagined. My insides were quickly shriveling up like an old balloon. Right in the middle of the SVJH hallway with the entire world going about its normal existence around me.

Elizabeth used to look at me like that. And not that long ago. It's funny how fast things can change. My face must've shown what I was feeling because she opened her mouth to stop me from leaving even before I knew I was going to. I didn't give her time to say anything, though. I turned on my heel and bolted before I had the chance to see Salvador throw his arm around her.

Elizabeth

"Blue!" I yelled over the noisy voices and slamming lockers that filled the hall. My heart was in my shoes after seeing his face. I started to take off after him, but it was pointless. He'd disappeared around the corner and was probably halfway to the other side of the school by now. I'd never have time to catch up with him and talk to him before homeroom.

School hadn't even officially started yet, and already this day was the worst.

I let out a long sigh and leaned back against the wall, feeling heavy all of a sudden. I couldn't believe that I was capable of making anyone feel like that. Especially someone I liked as much as I liked Blue. It was awful.

"You okay?"

I looked up to find Salvador standing in front of me, leaning on his crutches, his forehead all scrunched up in concern. My heart sped up at the sight of him, and I immediately felt awkward and flustered. I could tell my face was turning red, and I cleared my throat, stalling so my pulse would have a chance to slow down again. It was so weird, feeling like a giggly, crush-infected idiot around Salvador.

"I guess so," I said finally, pushing a stray hair back from my face and looking off down the hallway. I couldn't even look Salvador in the eye. What was he thinking about us—as in, him and me as more than friends? How was I supposed to act around him now?

"Would it help cheer you up if I slipped and fell off my crutches in some loud, comical, totally embarrassing way?" Salvador asked. "'Cause I could do that."

I laughed and finally looked up at him. Salvador grinned back, and my heart skipped a couple of dozen beats. I started to relax at the same time. This was still Sal. And his being there and looking at me with that glint in his eye—it made me feel perfectly happy. I couldn't believe one person could do that.

"That's okay," I told him, shaking my head. "But I might take you up on it later."

"Anytime," Salvador said in a voice that sent a chill down my spine. "The cafeteria would be prime. No better place for ultimate embarrassment potential."

"Thanks for the tip," I said. We were just

looking into each other's eyes, smiling, until Anna totally broke up the moment.

"Anyway . . . ," she said, giving me a meaningful glance. Anna was pretty much the only person, besides Jessica, of course, I'd told about what had happened between Salvador and me. She'd been supportive and really, really surprised. Now she just looked amused.

"Hey, guys." My locker partner, Brian Rainey, was walking down the hall toward us with his girlfriend, Kristin. "What's going on?"

"Hey," Anna said, simultaneously throwing a huge stack of books on the floor in front of my locker and pulling out her little planner. She uncapped her pink Hello Kitty pen and glanced around at us. "So since we're all here, we should get organized for the next *Zone* meeting," she said. "What's the game plan?"

As we started to fill Anna in on the plans for the rest of the week, I felt my smile start to fade. A *Zone* meeting? What was the point? Pretty soon I'd be gone, and then I'd never see another issue of the 'zine again.

Jessica

"Hey, guys!" I said overexcitedly as Damon and I approached Elizabeth, Salvador, Anna, Kristin, and Brian. They all seemed to be in the middle of planning something, but I didn't care. With this many people around, Damon would definitely get distracted and talk to someone else, and this awkward silence would be over.

"All right, I gotta go," Anna said, slapping a little notebook closed and grabbing a couple of books from a pile on the floor. "You'll get Sal's books, right, Liz?" she said with a wink.

Elizabeth rolled her eyes, and then Kristin and Anna walked off toward their homeroom.

"We should go too," Brian said to Damon.

Great! Take him! I thought. I needed some time away from Damon so I could rethink how I was going to handle this whole thing. I definitely couldn't tell him at school. Not when we were surrounded by people and could be interrupted at any second.

Jessica

"Okay," Damon said. He glanced at me, confused (who could blame him?), and took a step away. Just when I thought I was in the clear, he stopped and turned to look at me again. "Jess, do you want to hang out after school today?" he asked.

I looked at Elizabeth in a panic, and she nodded very discreetly. "Uh . . . okay," I said reluctantly. If we hung out after school, I would definitely have to tell him. There would be no room for excuses.

"Cool," he said. He touched my wrist and leaned over to give me a quick kiss on the cheek. Then he looked me directly in the eye with this very serious expression. I looked right back at him, hoping to show him that I wasn't a total flake.

"Cool," I repeated back to him. He smiled this supremely sweet smile. Then he turned and followed Brian down the hall and through the back doors.

"Ugh!" I groaned as soon as Damon was gone. I felt like my heart was being ripped out of my chest. "What am I going to do?"

Elizabeth gathered up Salvador's books, and the three of us started off down the hall together. "You're going to tell him," Elizabeth said, pushing all the books together into a neat pile to make them easier to carry.

Salvador was watching her shuffle his books

with this happy, googly-eyed look, and I almost puked. Enough of this lovey-dovey stuff. I was in the middle of a crisis situation.

"You guys, promise you won't tell Damon anything," I said, looking them each in the eye. "I want him to hear it from me."

"We won't say a word," Elizabeth said. Then she took a deep breath and let it out slowly. "But don't forget Blue knows too."

My stomach dropped like a bowling ball. "Omigod, Liz! You have to talk to him!" I said. "Blue and Damon are friends, and if Blue says anything—"

"I'll talk to him!" Elizabeth said, looking utterly miserable. "I'll talk to him as soon as I can."

At that moment the bell rang, and I looked at Elizabeth and Salvador. "You go," Salvador said to me. "I have a pass that says I can be late for class, and I'm sure that applies to the person who has to carry my books too."

"You sure?" I asked.

"Yeah, go," Elizabeth answered.

"Don't forget to talk to Blue," I said before turning and jogging off toward homeroom. All I could think of was how upset Damon would be if he found out my big news secondhand from the guy Elizabeth had dissed. He'd be devastated. I just hoped Elizabeth would get to Blue first.

Elizabeth

That afternoon I walked along the back of the library, glancing down each aisle of books, looking for Blue. It was perfectly quiet, and I was so tense, I felt like everyone in the place was watching me. I'd purposely waited until study hall to talk to him. If we were in the library, we'd be able to talk, but he wouldn't be able to yell at me if he felt the need. My palms were all sweaty, and I held my breath every time I came to the edge of a row of books.

Finally I found him in the second-to-last row at a big table. He was alone, and he had his back to me, which gave me a few seconds to get up the guts to go over there.

Don't hate me. Just don't hate me, I thought as I tiptoed up behind him.

When I got to the table, Blue sensed someone was there. He looked up at me and then looked right back down at the book he was reading. My stomach turned. He hadn't even blinked. There was a backpack on the table in front of the chair next to his. I slid it to the end of the table and sat down next to him.

"I know you don't want to talk to me, but I have to talk to you," I whispered, hoping he wouldn't just ignore me.

"So talk," Blue said, never taking his eyes off his book.

I wasn't going to let him get to me. I had to do this, for me, for him, and for Jessica. "Blue, I'm really sorry about everything that's happened—"

"It's really no big deal," Blue said, shifting and sitting way back in his chair. "So don't try to make a big deal out of it."

I pulled back a little, sitting up straight. "If it's no big deal, then why are you so mad at me?"

"I'm not," he said, forcing a smile and glancing at me for less than a second.

I sighed. "Blue, I wish you would talk to me so I could figure out how to . . . I don't know. . . . I just want us to be friends."

"Are you and Sal going out?" he asked firmly, looking me directly in the eye. His blue eyes were angry but also hopeful somehow.

I was so surprised by his direct question, I didn't even know what to say. Apparently my silence was enough of an answer for Blue.

"I don't get it," he said. "I thought things were cool with us."

29

Elizabeth

"They were," I said, hearing the sound of desperation in my voice. "It's not like we were having problems and Sal swooped in on me or something. . . . It just . . . happened." I knew it wasn't much of an explanation, but it was the only one I had.

"It doesn't make sense," Blue said, gripping his book. "How could things have changed that fast? And you told me it was a bad time because you guys are moving and everything . . . but then why isn't it a bad time for you to get together with Sal?"

He had me there. How was I supposed to tell him that it just felt right with Salvador? That what Salvador and I had together was worth having for a little while? It sounded awful, even to me.

Blue was just staring at me, waiting for an answer.

"I don't know what to say." My eyes filled with tears. I'd been crying so much lately, you'd think I'd be all dried out.

"Well, when you think of something, I'll be around," Blue said, standing up and shoving his books into his backpack. He turned and stalked away, and I just let him go. What else was I supposed to do? There was nothing I could say to make him feel better. There was nothing I could say even to make me feel better. I was evil.

As soon as he was gone, I folded my arms in front of me and rested my head on them. A couple of tears rolled out of my eyes and splattered onto the redwood tabletop. I sniffled and tried to get control of myself. The last thing I needed was to have a sobbing fit in the middle of the library. Suddenly I felt someone standing over me. I sniffled again and wiped my eyes with the back of my hands. When I looked up, I expected to find one of the librarians ready to scold me for being noisy or something. But what I saw made my whole body go cold.

It was Damon. And he did not look happy.

He slowly sat down next to me and pulled the backpack I'd shoved aside over to him. Before he said a word, I understood everything. He'd been sitting with Blue, and he'd been in the stacks while Blue and I talked. He'd heard everything. Every . . . single . . . thing.

Jessica was going to kill me.

"You're moving?" Damon said finally. He was holding the library book in his hand so tightly, his knuckles had turned white.

For the second time in the last few minutes, I had no idea what to say.

Damon

"Well? Is it true or isn't it?"

I stayed there for a few long seconds, waiting for an answer, but when Elizabeth didn't say anything, I pretty much jumped out of the chair, grabbed the extra bathroom pass, and took off after Blue. Somebody was going to have to tell me what was going on. He was already at the other end of the hall, heading for the bathroom himself.

"Blue!" I yell-whispered, jogging after him.

He stopped and turned to wait for me, adjusting his backpack. He looked really mad and tense, and I had a feeling he wasn't in the mood to talk. I guess something had happened between Elizabeth and Salvador, and now Blue was out of the picture. I felt bad for him, but right now I could only focus on one thing. My brain was still processing what I'd overheard and refusing to believe it.

"What's up, man?" Blue asked, eyeing me as I stopped in front of him, my sneakers squeaking loudly.

"Not much," I said, even though a lot was up. "Look, did I hear you right back there? Are the Wakefields . . . moving?"

Blue's mouth hung open a little in surprise. He shifted his weight from one foot to the other. "Dude, Jessica didn't tell you?"

My heart squeezed. So I wasn't the only one who realized that the fact Jessica hadn't told me about this was completely wrong. "No," I said, trying not to look as pathetic as I felt. "What do you know about it . . . the move, I mean?"

"Well, all I know is that they're leaving pretty soon and they're moving to Utah," Blue said, rubbing his forehead.

"Utah?" I repeated, my eyebrows shooting up. She might as well be moving to Brazil. "Why would they move to Utah?"

Blue sighed and shifted again. He was obviously not in the mood to talk. "I don't know, man," he said. "Something about their dad's job. Look, I'm really sorry, Damon. But I gotta go. Can we talk later?" He took a step backward, but not toward the bathroom—toward the back door.

"Yeah," I said, watching him shove through the big wooden door and out into the sun. Apparently he was cutting the rest of study hall. But that was pretty much the last thing on my mind.

I just stood there, in the middle of the hall,

clutching the big wooden bathroom pass and feeling like someone had just shoved me into a bottomless pit.

This move thing definitely explained why Jessica had been acting so weird lately, so she wasn't going to break up with me. That was a relief. But once I got past the relief, which was pretty quickly, I started to feel really horrible. Jessica moving away was a lot worse than her breaking up with me. I'd probably never see her again. At least if we broke up and she was still here, there'd always be a chance . . . and I'd still get to see her.

I leaned back against the cold brick wall and looked up at the ceiling. This sad, confused, scared feeling filled me. Never seeing Jessica again. I couldn't even imagine it. Never watch her walking toward me in the cafeteria with that amazing smile on her face. Never see her wrestling with my sisters again. Never watch her chewing on her pencil as she tried to figure out her math homework. It didn't seem possible.

Maybe that was partly because I hadn't even officially heard about it yet. Like, from Jessica. Why hadn't she told me? How could she let me walk around, totally ignorant, while everyone else obviously knew what was going on? I felt like an idiot. I felt . . . betrayed.

Judging from that conversation between Elizabeth and Blue, Blue had known about this for days. And he and Elizabeth weren't even going out! I pushed myself away from the wall. What was Jessica going to do? Wait until her family got settled and then send me a postcard?

Didn't I matter to her at all?

A poem by Blue

I've waited for the perfect wave
the perfect sunset
the perfect wind

I've tried to find the perfect orange
the perfect milk shake
the perfect jam

I've worked to write the perfect paper
the perfect essay
the perfect poem

Then I found the perfect girl
and learned one small thing

Perfection isn't everything I thought it would be

Elizabeth

"She's going to kill me. . . . She's going to kill me. . . . She's going to hurt me, then kill me. . . ."

I was muttering under my breath as I raced through the halls of SVJH, looking for Jessica. Everyone that I passed must have thought I'd lost my mind. If only they knew everything I was dealing with, I'm sure they would have just felt sorry for me instead of giving me those frightened looks.

"Hey, Liz! Do you . . ."

Salvador was trying to flag me down, but I couldn't stop to talk to him at the moment. I had to tell Jessica what had happened with Damon.

I took the corner before Jessica's locker way too fast and almost fell. There she was. Standing at her locker, totally innocent, not knowing her own sister had stabbed her in the back. I sucked wind and ran through the crowded hall, focusing on her blond hair, totally identical to mine.

37

Elizabeth

She wasn't going to kill me. She was my sister! My twin! She'd understand. I was just doing what I was supposed to—talking to Blue. How was I supposed to know Damon was an eavesdropper?

"Jess!" I said, just before I basically ran into her.

"Ow!" she said, rolling her eyes with a laugh. "What's your deal?"

"I'm . . . sorry," I said, trying to catch my breath and talk at the same time. "Listen! I . . . have . . . to . . . talk . . . Damon . . ."

"I have to talk to you about Damon too," Jessica said nonchalantly, as if I wasn't standing there gasping for air. "I've decided I'm definitely going to tell him after school today." She nodded with determination and slammed her locker shut.

"That'swhatIwantedtotalktoyouabout!" I said in one big breath.

Jessica's eyebrows twisted in confusion. "Huh?"

At that very moment Damon appeared out of nowhere and came up behind Jessica. He just stared at me, directly in the eye, and suddenly I completely lost the ability to talk.

"Hey," he said.

Jessica's eyes widened, and she turned to face him. "Hi!" she said brightly. "How long have you been standing there?"

I knew she was worried that he'd overheard her telling me that she had something to tell him. Little did she know it really didn't matter what he'd heard just now. He'd already heard it all.

"So, we still hanging out?" Damon asked, stuffing his hands in the front pockets of his wrinkled khakis.

"Yeah!" Jessica said, way too eagerly. "Why wouldn't we be? I mean, I have to talk to you about something."

"Then let's go," Damon said. He didn't seem too happy, but he was acting fairly normal for Damon. Why didn't he seem more upset?

"'Kay," Jessica said. She lifted her backpack from the floor and onto her shoulder, then turned to me and forced a smile. "Bye, Liz!"

"Bye, guys," I muttered, feeling totally confused. Jessica shot me a you're-losing-it look, then turned and walked off with Damon.

I leaned back against the wall and sank to the floor, suddenly too exhausted to move. This had not been a good day. And now I had to go to a *Zone* meeting. All I really wanted to do was curl up in bed and be miserable.

Jessica

Silence.

I was trying to come up with something to say to Damon, something to just start a normal conversation that could then turn into a serious conversation. But I was freaking out so bad, I could hardly remember how to speak English. We'd been sitting in a booth at Vito's for fifteen minutes, and so far I'd mentally put off telling him the big news no less than three times. First I thought I'd wait till we got a table, then I put it off until we ordered. Then, for some reason, I thought it would be logical to wait until we got our drinks. Maybe so that I'd have something to fiddle with—I hadn't stopped playing with my straw since the waitress had put my Sprite down in front of me.

Now I was putting it off until we got our food. Yep. The second that waitress put the pizza down in front of us, I was going to open my mouth and break the news. No ifs, ands, or buts.

The waitress walked over and placed a steaming-hot extra-cheese-and-pepperoni pizza on the table.

My stomach turned. Damon dug right in. Suddenly waiting for the food seemed like a bad idea. I mean, who wanted to hear bad news while they were trying to digest all that dairy and grease?

"Wait!" I blurted out as Damon lifted a heaping slice to his mouth. He froze. His mouth was open, and there was a huge chunk of cheese sliding off the side of his slice.

"I have something to tell you before you eat that," I said, my sweaty palms trying to grip the vinyl seat at my sides.

Damon lowered the slice back down to his paper plate, never taking his eyes off my face. "Okay," he said.

"Okay," I repeated, pushing myself back in the seat. This was going to be okay. He would be upset, but he'd adjust, and then everything would be fine. "So . . . the other day, my father came home and he—"

"Hi, guys!"

Oh no.

It was Kristin. I looked up, and there she was, standing next to our booth, all smiles in a pink sweater and a ponytail. And where there was Kristin, there was usually . . .

Lacey. Who had just walked in and seen Kristin was talking to us. After making a disgusted face, she was now on her way over to our table.

Jessica

"That looks so good," Kristin said, eyeing our pizza.

"Yeah, we don't know yet," Damon said, indicating his untouched slice.

"Well, enjoy," Lacey said, coming up, hooking her arm through Kristin's, and pulling her away.

Please just sit on the other side of the room, I urged them silently. *Please, please, please . . .* I really wanted to tell Kristin my news too. But that would have to wait until after I'd talked to Damon. And how could I tell Damon if Kristin and Lacey were anywhere near us?

That was when I felt them plop down in the booth right behind me. Perfection.

"So, you were going to tell me something?" Damon said, leaning back in his seat.

I just sighed and stared down at my lap. I had to tell him. I knew I had to. But now Lacey and Kristin were going to overhear the whole heart-wrenching thing.

And the whole school would know within five seconds.

Damon

I watched Jessica for a few seconds, waiting for her to say something. I'd actually been watching her for more than twenty minutes, waiting for her to say something, but so far she'd been practically mute all afternoon. I couldn't believe this. Why wasn't she telling me? Why did she feel like she had to hide the fact that her family was moving? It was so . . . weird.

"Jess?" I said.

"Forget it," she answered with a wave of her hand. She didn't even look up. She was busy picking at a rip in the vinyl seat.

"Ooookay." I picked up my slice again and took a big bite. If she didn't want to tell me, it wasn't my problem. It wasn't like I was going to sit there and help her out. She'd had plenty of chances to tell me, and she hadn't. What did she think I was going to do, yell at her?

Actually, at this point, that was kind of what I felt like doing.

"Damon?" she said.

Damon

I sighed. "Yeah?" I mumbled through a mouthful of food.

"Okay, here's the thing. . . ."

She trailed off again. I kept eating. She squirmed in her seat.

"Uh . . . this is really hard," she said, still staring down.

Just say it, I thought. *Just get it over with and say it.*

"Okay, I'm just going to say it," she said.

There you go, I thought.

"I'm moving to Utah," she blurted out finally.

"What?" Kristin exclaimed. Lacey turned completely around in her seat and peeked over the bench, looking over at me.

Jessica just kept going. "My family's moving. To Utah. We're moving, and that's what I wanted to tell you." She let out a long sigh like she was totally relieved.

I just kept eating. Jessica finally snuck a glance at me, and her forehead wrinkled up in confusion.

"Jess—" Kristin said.

"Kris, I'll call you later and tell you everything, okay?" Jessica said, throwing an apologetic look at Kristin and then turning to gape at me as if I'd sprouted a huge amount of nose hair or something. "Damon? Did you hear what I just said? I'm moving."

Wow. Once she got started, she couldn't seem

to stop saying it. "Yeah, I already knew," I said matter-of-factly.

Jessica's mouth dropped open, and her face got even paler than it already was. "You . . . knew? How?"

"Elizabeth," I said, taking another bite out of my slice.

"What?" she screeched. "She told you?" Her cheeks were suddenly redder than the sauce on the pizza, and she looked like she was going to crawl out of her skin. "I'm going to—"

"Before you freak out, Elizabeth didn't tell me," I said calmly. "I overheard her talking to Blue in study hall."

"Oh," Jessica said. She swallowed and took some time to process everything. "So, if you knew, why didn't you tell me?"

That was when I almost lost it. "Why didn't I tell you?" I said, finally putting down my slice and looking her in the eye. "How long have you known about this? How long has Blue and everyone else known about this? How long have I been walking around as, like, almost the only person, besides Kristin, apparently, who doesn't know my girlfriend is moving?"

Jessica scowled, pursing her lips. I could see tears start to fill her eyes, but I told myself not to care. I was mad, and it wasn't my fault. "Is that all you care about?" she said, crossing her arms over her chest. "The fact that you didn't know? Do you even care that I'm leaving? I mean, you seem to be taking the news kind of well."

"I'd be taking it a lot better if I'd heard it from my girlfriend," I spat back, feeling my own face get hot.

"I . . . I wanted to tell you," Jessica said finally, her voice cracking. "I was just waiting for the right time. I didn't want you to get hurt." She let out a loud breath and looked at me warily.

I stared right back, hardening my eyes. She didn't want me to get hurt? Well, she'd done a really bad job of keeping that from happening.

"You know what hurts me the most?" I said slowly. I've never been very good at expressing my feelings, but if I didn't try to tell her how I felt, I would explode right there. "It's like you didn't trust me. Like you didn't trust me to . . . be there for you or whatever. After everything . . ." She bit her lip, and I took a deep breath and let it out slowly. "That's what hurts."

Jessica

I was sitting in the middle of Vito's Pizza, feeling like I was being torn apart from all sides. I understood why Damon was mad. I really did. But didn't he care about me at all?

"Damon, I'm really sorry about how you found out," I said quietly, trying hard to keep myself from bursting into tears. I could tell Kristin and Lacey were listening to every single word we said, and I was completely uncomfortable. All I wanted to do was run out the front door, go home, and hide. But I had to focus. I couldn't lose Damon now. I'd never get through the next few weeks without him. "I'm sorry, okay?" I said desperately.

"Whatever," Damon said with a shrug. He was still eating his pizza as if nothing was going on. As if my whole world wasn't crumbling down around me.

"Why are you acting like this?" I blurted out.

"Like what?" Damon said, his face totally blank.

Like the biggest jerk on the face of the planet, I thought. But I had a feeling saying that wasn't

47

going to help. I bit my tongue. I'd never been good at controlling myself during arguments, but this was too important.

"Like you don't care about me leaving," I said as evenly as possible. One tear spilled over onto my cheek, and I wiped it away quickly.

Damon just looked down at his plate and slowly took another bite of pizza. I couldn't take it anymore. This was the most humiliating experience of my entire life. I stood up quickly and jammed my knee on the underside of the table, knocking over my Sprite and soaking the paper plates. My knee was killing me, but I barely noticed.

"You know what?" I said, tears now freely spilling over. "If it doesn't matter to you that I'm moving, maybe we should just break up right now. I'm going to be gone at the end of the school year anyway. And that's not that far away."

Damon shrugged. I felt like my heart was shattering slowly. "If that's what you want."

"Yeah, that's what I want," I said, even though it absolutely wasn't. Why couldn't I just wake up from this nightmare and have my caring, cool boyfriend back?

I just glared at him for a second, and when it became clear he wasn't going to say anything else, I turned and ran out of Vito's. Suddenly I didn't care if I never saw that place again.

Damon

The second Jessica split, I realized I still had a hunk of cheese, pepperoni, and crust in my mouth. It took all my effort just to finish chewing it and swallow. I stared down at the pizza in front of me. What a waste. What a waste this whole day had been. When I'd woken up that morning, it had been just like any other day. I'd walked into the shower with my eyes still closed, fed my sisters, scarfed a bowl of Fruity Pebbles, and gone to school.

Now Jessica was leaving, we'd basically just broken up, and I'd never been more angry and confused in my life. Everything had changed.

Suddenly I felt like I was being watched. I looked left and scanned the restaurant, but there was nothing. Then I caught a glimpse of Lacey's curly brown hair out of the corner of my eye. I looked up, and she and Kristin were both kneeling on Lacey's seat, glaring down at me. "What did I do?" I asked, my face burning.

Damon

"Are you kidding me?" Lacey demanded, her eyes flashing.

She might as well have slapped me in the face and dumped a bucket of cold water over my head. It was like I'd been snapped out of a dream. If Lacey was taking Jessica's side, I must have been really, really wrong.

I jumped up and tore out of Vito's. I had to catch up with Jessica. I had no idea what I was going to say, but I had to catch her. I ran across the small parking lot, but when I hit the sidewalk and looked both ways, Jessica was nowhere in sight. My stomach turned and twisted. This was not good.

I put my hands on my hips and took a second to catch my breath. Maybe it was better this way. I mean, there was no way to fix this. Jessica was leaving, and that was that. It wasn't like I could make her stay. I didn't want her to hate me, but maybe we were better off with a clean break.

Then I remembered I hadn't paid for the food. Looking back at Vito's, I rubbed my forehead and then shuffled back toward the building, telling myself I was right. This was the right thing. It really was.

So why did I still feel like I was going to barf?

Kristin's Journal

*I can't believe Jessica and Elizabeth are ac-
tually moving. To Utah. Why Utah? What do
they even have there? Sand? What's sand without the ocean? Pointless, basically.*

*I'm really going to miss Jessica. She's be-
come such a good friend this year. I never
thought I'd be as close to anyone as I am to
Lacey, but I really think I am with Jessica—
just in a totally different way. I tell them both
everything, I just get entirely different feedback
from each of them. And I'm really going to miss
that. It makes life a lot more interesting.*

*Besides, I love Lacey, but come on, she can be
a pain in the butt sometimes.*

*I'm going to miss having a somewhat low-
maintenance friend like Jessica.*

What am I going to do without her?

Lacey's Journal

I can't believe Jessica's moving. But Utah is, like, the perfect place for her. She's so pure and perfect and innocent, she'll probably fit right in. The whole state is probably full of blond, blue-eyed, sweet mama's girls. The Wakefields will blend right in. Or <u>bland</u> right in.

But with Jessica gone, I won't have anyone to mock anymore. Okay, I'm sure there are plenty of sorry souls at SVJH just waiting to become the target of my fabulous wit, but still . . . Jessica was so perfect for it. Why? Because she thinks she's so great, but it's so easy to pick her apart. The girl crumbles so easily. Even when she tries not to show it, it's so obvious I'm getting to her. It takes, like, no effort.

What am I going to do without her?

Elizabeth

"We got more reader mail for the last issue than any other issue yet," Anna said proudly, glancing down at her notebook. She looked up and grinned at Brian, Salvador, and me. "Must've been that in-depth report on the secret lives of teachers that Ronald submitted."

Salvador and Brian laughed. Ronald Rheece is Jessica's nerdy locker partner, and he's one of those people who's funny even though he doesn't mean to be—just because he takes everything so seriously. Which is exactly why his teacher story was so funny.

But I was in no mood to be amused. I just sighed and kept staring off at the map of the United States that was hanging on the wall across the room. Utah was like this big, pink zit just staring back at me. Why Utah? There must've been a million jobs my dad could have applied for in southern California. Why couldn't he have just found one in Sweet Valley or Big Mesa or Los Angeles? LA wasn't that far away.

Elizabeth

Even San Diego or Santa Barbara would have been fine. I could've taken the bus back to see my friends. But Utah? Once we moved there, it was either going to take a miracle or a lottery win for me to ever get back here.

"That sounds awesome, Sal," Anna was saying. "Do you think you can get that story ready by the next issue?"

I blinked, realizing I had no idea what story idea Salvador had just pitched. I was completely spacing. But the realization didn't stop me from glaring at Utah. Maybe if I tried hard enough, I could obliterate it from the map with my brain waves.

"I have an idea," Brian said, pushing himself up straight in his chair. "Now that we're getting toward the end of the year, I was thinking it would be cool to do a look back. You know, talk to people about how much everything has changed since the rezoning."

"Cool." Anna scrawled some notes down in her notebook.

Brian's right, I thought. *Everything has changed so much. At the beginning of the year if you'd ever told me I'd have friends like the ones at this table, I would have laughed in your face.* All I could think about back then was how much I was going to miss Todd and Maria and everyone at SVMS. Now I'd had so many new crushes, Todd was a distant memory, and I barely ever spoke to Maria anymore. Anna and Salvador were the best friends I could have ever asked for. And I was never going to see them again.

I sighed again. Loudly.

"Liz? Liz, are you okay?"

I turned my head slowly and looked at Anna. "Huh?"

She cracked a sympathetic smile. "I've only said your name about ten times."

One glance at Salvador and Brian told me she wasn't exaggerating. Salvador was looking at me all concerned, and Brian, knowing nothing about the move, was obviously confused. I was never this out of it at a *Zone* meeting.

"What's wrong?" Brian asked, fiddling with his notepad. "You don't like the idea?"

"No, I love the idea," I said, attempting to sit up but only making it about halfway. I glanced at Anna and Salvador, asking them with my eyes if they thought I should just tell Brian what was up. They both nodded with encouraging smiles.

"I'm sorry I'm so out of it, Brian," I said, looking down at the blond wood grain of the table-top. "It's just, I just found out last week that my family's moving."

"Oh," Brian said slowly. "Where?"

Elizabeth

"Utah," Anna, Salvador, and I all answered in monotone unison.

"Oh," Brian said again. "That stinks."

We all sat there for a few minutes in silence while Brian's last words hung in the air. It seemed like there was nothing else to say. Brian had wrapped up the situation in a nutshell.

Brian's Journal

I can't believe Elizabeth and Jessica are actually leaving. When Elizabeth told me, I had no idea what to say. And that doesn't happen a lot. It's just . . . I'm not great friends with either Elizabeth or Jessica, but I know school isn't going to be the same without them. They're just fun to have around. And <u>Zone</u> meetings are going to be so weird without Elizabeth there. The four of us go really well together. I wonder if it'll still work without her.

And then there's Jessica. Kristin is going to freak when she finds out Jessica is leaving. I don't know what I would do if one of my best friends moved away. Everything would just shift. Like, I know Kristin calls Jessica all the time, and they go to the mall together and stuff. And that person is just not going to be there anymore. It's going to be weird for her.

I know I pitched an article for <u>Zone</u> about how good the changes at the beginning of the year turned out to be, but the truth is, I hate changes.

Salvador

After Elizabeth told Brian about the big move, the *Zone* meeting was pretty much . . . well, a dead *Zone,* actually. Anna tried to keep it going, but no one was in the mood. Finally we ended up talking about this stupid history exam we have coming up while Elizabeth went back to staring at Utah like she wished someone would just blow the place up.

Finally it was ten to four. My grandmother would be picking me up out front soon, and with my crutches it would take me a while to get out there. I suggested we call it a day, and everyone practically jumped out of their chairs.

"So, Liz, when exactly are you moving?" Brian asked as we made our way out the front doors of the school. He held the door open for me so I could maneuver through.

"Pretty much right after the school year ends," Elizabeth said, sounding tired. She adjusted her hold on my books, and I immediately felt bad. Tomorrow I'd bring my big backpack so I could carry all my books at once. "They haven't set an exact date yet. In a way, I don't even want to know."

"Wow," Brian said.

Yeah, wow. In just a few weeks Elizabeth would be gone.

"Do you guys know what your school's going to be like yet?" Brian asked as we slowly descended the steps.

"No," Elizabeth said.

"How about your house?" Brian asked.

She sighed. "I don't think we have one yet."

"What about—"

"Did anyone catch that Dodgers game yesterday?" I blurted out, leaning on my good leg and turning to face them. "That was some serious pitching, huh?"

I hadn't even seen the Dodgers game. I didn't even think the Dodgers had played. I just wanted Brian to stop grilling Elizabeth. I'm sure he didn't mean anything by it, but it was obvious to the world that she was upset. Or at least it was obvious to me.

"Uh . . . no," Brian said, flushing. I knew he took the hint, and I shot him a look telling him it was okay. Elizabeth was staring off into space again anyway. Just then, Brian's mom pulled up in her minivan. He headed to the car, and we all waved, not really knowing what else to say.

"There's my mom," Anna muttered, nodding at the edge of the parking lot, then glancing from Elizabeth to me and back again. I guess she realized there was nothing she could do to cheer Elizabeth up at this point. "I'll see you guys tomorrow."

"Bye," Elizabeth said distractedly.

"Later," I said, lifting my chin.

When they were finally gone, I looked at Elizabeth, and she forced a smile back at me. It was so weird. Considering we'd just recently gone from being friends to being . . . whatever we were now, you'd think we'd be all awkward and silly around each other. I'm a stumbling idiot on a good regular day, so technically I should have been falling all over myself. But all I could think about was whether or not she was okay. At least it made it easier not to focus on my pounding heart and sweaty palms.

"So . . . you wanna come over and watch some TV or something?" I asked, gripping the padded rungs on my crutches. "I think the Doña's going to try a new cookie recipe today."

Elizabeth sighed. "It's tempting . . . but I really think I should just go home," she said, looking off in the direction she would walk to get there. "Maybe a nice, long walk will help me clear my head."

Okay, so I'd be lying if I said I wasn't disappointed that she didn't want to come. I wanted to spend every second I could with her before she left, and part of me wished she felt the same way. But I couldn't hold it against her. I knew she had a lot on her mind.

The Doña's car pulled into the parking lot. "There's my ride," I said.

Elizabeth smiled and stepped over to me, adjusting my books again. "Thanks for the offer," she said. Then she stood up on her tiptoes and kissed me on the cheek. I must have turned about a million shades of red.

"Thanks . . . I mean . . . anytime . . . I mean . . ."

Elizabeth laughed. It was really good to see her laugh.

"You know what I mean," I said finally.

The car pulled to a stop in front of us, and Elizabeth walked over and opened the back door. "Hi, Doña!" she said, placing my books on the floor of the car.

"Hello, Elizabeth!" the Doña said giddily. I knew she'd seen that kiss, and I knew I was in for it. The Doña loved Elizabeth almost as much as she loved a good bean dip.

"Thanks, Liz," I said as I tossed my crutches into the car. "I swear, tomorrow you won't have to play Sal's servant anymore."

"Yeah, I think my arms stretched about a foot today," she joked, shaking out her arms.

"Very funny," I said. We shared a long look and smile, then I lowered myself into the car and closed the door. I lifted my hand, and Elizabeth waved as the Doña pulled the car away.

"So, Salvador, that was a very sweet little kiss," the Doña started in right away. "What did my grandson do to deserve such a sweet kiss?"

I turned in my seat to watch Elizabeth as she started to make her way to the sidewalk, my heart pounding like crazy. She was the most beautiful girl in the entire world. And she had kissed me. Of her own free will. At least, I was pretty sure no one was paying her off.

"I don't know, Doña," I said quietly. "I have no idea."

Jessica

Normally I like being around my family. Steven gets on my nerves sometimes, and when my parents are being too parental, it's not so great, but on a normal day I really like the people. Monday night was not normal. We were all sitting at the dinner table, silently pretending like nothing was wrong, and I felt like I was about to crawl out of my skin.

I couldn't even look at my father, who was the only person who had even tried to start a conversation all night. Every time he spoke, I gripped my fork so hard, I thought it was going to bend right there in my hand. All I could think was, *It's your fault. It's your fault. It's your fault.* Damon and I had broken up, and it was all my father's fault. I was never going to speak to him again.

The silence at the table was completely unnatural. I kept pushing my spaghetti around on my plate until it was formed into a perfect circle with a hole in the middle like a doughnut.

Jessica

Elizabeth was trying to look like she was eating, and Steven was chowing down like my mom had been starving him for weeks. (That was the difference between Steven and me. When he was upset, he ate everything in sight. When I was upset, I couldn't even look at food.) All I could hear was the sound of his chewing and swallowing. I couldn't take it anymore. When was this torture going to end?

"Kids, is everything okay?" my father asked finally, placing his silverware down on the table.

There I went again, gripping my fork. *Yeah, Dad, everything's fab!* I thought. *When do we start packing?* I scowled down at my plate. Steven grunted. I felt Elizabeth glance at me as if she was waiting for me to talk. Not likely.

"Yeah, Dad," she said. "Everything's fine."

"Good," he said, leaning his elbows on the table. "Because I wanted to talk to you a little bit more about Utah, and I—"

"Omigod!" I blurted out, standing up and pushing back my chair. I was so angry, the entire room was out of focus, but I could tell my whole family was looking at me in shock. I didn't care.

"Is that all you can talk about? Utah?" I shouted, my hands balling into fists. "I guess you're going to tell us how great and fabulous and perfect it's going to be again, right? Well, you know what? I think it's going to be horrible. I think it's going to be the worst thing that ever happened to me."

"Jessica—"

"Oh, wait!" I said, ignoring my dad's stern tone. I couldn't have stopped myself if I tried. "The worst thing that ever happened to me already happened. This afternoon. Yeah. Damon and I broke up. Wanna know why?" I said, glaring at my father. "Because of you! Damon hates me, and it's all your fault! You don't care about anybody! Did you ever even think about the rest of us? No. And now my life is over all because you have to have some stupid job in Utah!"

I turned, ran out of the dining room, and took the stairs two at a time. I slammed the door to my room and turned the lock, even though I was strictly forbidden to ever lock my door. I didn't care about my parents' stupid rules anymore. I didn't care about anything they had to say.

Elizabeth

I'd heard that expression "You could cut the tension in the air with a knife," but I'd never understood it until the moment I heard Jessica's door slam. The rest of my family just sat at the table, frozen like extremely tense statues. My father's mouth was set in such a grim line, you could barely see his lips. All I could think about was the fact that Jessica and Damon had broken up. No wonder she'd been hiding in her room all afternoon. I'd wanted to find out what was up, but I'd been pretty out of it myself. Now I felt so bad for her. I knew her heart was broken, and it made mine feel broken too.

"I'm going to go talk to her," my dad said, starting up from his seat.

I jumped up, scraping my chair back loudly. "No, I'll go." If my dad went up there, there'd just be a lot of yelling and crying, and that wasn't going to help anyone. I think my father realized that too because he just sat down again. My mom gave me a long, sad look, and I knew she was hoping I could fix things a little. I hoped so too.

I went upstairs and tried Jessica's door, but it was locked. Not a good sign. "Jess? Can I come in?"

I heard the clicking of the lock, and the door swung open. Jessica jumped back onto her bed and hugged a pillow to her chest. There were crumpled tissues strewn all over the room, and her bedspread was a twisted mess. Her face was soaked with tears, and you could feel the misery in the room.

"God, Jess, I am so sorry about Damon," I said, sitting down on her bed. "What happened?"

"It doesn't matter," she said through her sobs. I pulled a tissue out of the box next to me and handed it to her. "He hates me. He doesn't care that I'm leaving."

"That's not true, and you know it," I said, pushing her hair back from her face. "I guess you heard what happened in the library."

"Yes," she said, blowing her nose loudly. She looked at me, her eyes hard. "How could you tell him?"

"I didn't tell him. He overheard me," I said, my insides twisting. I'd seen Jessica upset before, but I couldn't remember the last time she'd been like this. Damon must have been really harsh with her.

"What happened?" I asked again.

Elizabeth

She sniffled and toyed with the tissue in her lap. "He was really mad at me for not telling him. Really mad. And I kept telling him I was sorry, but he was just such a jerk about it." She took a deep breath, and it came out all ragged. "So I told him if he didn't care, we should just break up, and do you know what he said?" She looked up at me, her eyes bright with tears. "He said, 'Whatever.' Can you even believe that?"

Actually, I couldn't believe it. That didn't sound like Damon at all. Which could only mean one thing. "I'm sure he was just hurt. He didn't really mean that," I said. "He was just getting over the shock of the whole thing. Maybe tomorrow you should just apologize again and—"

"Me?" Jessica blurted out, pressing her hand against her chest. "I should apologize to him? No way. I think it's his turn."

I sighed and rubbed my eyes. I had to agree with her. Why didn't Damon understand that Jessica was going through something awful? Couldn't he just put his own feelings aside and be there for her? Suddenly I felt completely exhausted. Every single limb of my body weighed nine hundred pounds.

"Everything hurts," Jessica said quietly. "I can't deal with this. There isn't one single thing I can think of to make myself feel better."

I knew what she meant, but I also knew that what had happened downstairs hadn't helped anyone. I bet it felt good while she was yelling—getting it all out—but now I knew we all just felt worse.

"You know, there is one thing you can do," I said slowly.

"What?" Jessica said in a sarcastic tone. I knew she knew what I was going to say, but I said it anyway.

"You can apologize to Dad."

Jessica snorted, and her eyes filled with tears again. "I hate him," she said.

"No, you don't," I responded. "I know everything stinks right now, but Dad does care about us. You know he does."

She took a deep breath and looked me in the eye. "Yeah, I know." Then she wiped her eyes with a tissue and sighed. "I just want this day to be over with."

I reached over and put my arms around her. She squeezed me back tightly. "I know exactly what you mean."

The only problem was, this whole thing wasn't going to go away with a little sleep. It wasn't going to go away . . . ever.

Jessica

Elizabeth walked downstairs in front of me as if she was trying to be my shield or something. I was kind of glad she did it. My dad was probably really angry and really disappointed, and I didn't want to see his face. Not that Elizabeth could stop that from happening. It was just good to have her there.

I could hear dishes clanking in the kitchen, and I knew they were clearing the table. When we walked into the dining room, my dad was just coming back in from the kitchen to get more plates and stuff. His sleeves were rolled up, he'd ditched his tie, and his shirt was unbuttoned at the neck. He froze when he saw us. He looked really, really tired.

"Hey . . . ," I said.

"Jessica," he said. I could tell from his voice he was still mad but trying not to sound mad. He's not the best actor.

"I'm really sorry, Dad," I said. Just then my brother walked in from the kitchen, took one look at us, turned around, and disappeared again.

"I know," my dad said, sighing so long, it seemed like his chest was collapsing. He looked me in the eye, and I bit my lip. "I do care about how you feel, honey," he said.

"I know," I answered. I didn't know what else to say. I felt so bad and sorry, but I still felt angry and disappointed. It made me nostalgic for last week, when my biggest worry was the fear of failing my English test.

"It's going to be fine. It really is. I promise," Dad said.

My eyes filled with tears. Elizabeth, who was standing a little off to my side, took a step closer to me. "I know." It seemed like that was all I could remember how to say.

Then my dad walked over to me and put his arms around me and Elizabeth, holding us tight. I could smell his aftershave, and his starched shirt felt a little scratchy on my cheek. My dad had smelled and felt the same way my entire life, and it was kind of comforting. Like I suddenly realized no matter where we were, I'd always have Elizabeth, Dad would always be the same, Steven would always be immature, and my mom would still be there for us.

"I love you girls," my dad said.

"We love you too," we said back, our voices all muffled.

When he let go, I felt like I'd never been so tired in my life. Elizabeth let out a huge yawn, and my dad chuckled.

"Maybe we should all go to bed early tonight," he said, ruffling our hair.

Sounded like a plan to me. I could have fallen asleep just standing there. I guess constant emotional craziness takes a lot out of a girl. If that was the case, it seemed like I'd be doing a lot of sleeping over the next few weeks.

Bethel's Journal

Jessica is moving. I can't believe it. I just got off the phone with Kristin, and it took me about fifteen minutes to even move. She overheard Jessica telling Damon about it at Vito's today. I just really can't believe it. And I can't believe she didn't tell me herself. But then, she didn't tell Kristin either. I guess she wanted to tell Damon first so he wouldn't find out from anyone else. Still, I wish I'd known what she was going through.

I never really had a best friend until Jessica. I know it sounds pathetic—thirteen and no best friends. But I don't know, it's hard to believe, but I've always been kind of shy, and everybody took that to mean I was mean. So then I would act kind of tough, and that meant no best friends for me. Jessica was the first person who could deal with me long enough to become a real, true friend. And now she's leaving.

Track is going to be so lame without her.

Everything is going to be so lame without her.

Jessica

The next morning Elizabeth and I promised ourselves we would be positive. Mom was right. There was no reason to be totally miserable for the rest of our time in Sweet Valley. So when I got out of the shower, I put on my favorite outfit—a red fitted T-shirt and a funky colorful skirt with knee-high boots—and Elizabeth and I practically skipped to school. We didn't feel like skipping, but we figured if we acted happy, maybe we could fool ourselves and we'd become happy. We were going to pretend absolutely nothing was wrong.

But the second we walked into school, it was obvious that wasn't going to be possible. Everyone was staring at us as we walked through the halls. People were whispering, and as we walked, gradually pulling closer and closer to each other, I caught little pieces of hushed conversations.

"I feel so bad for them. . . ."

"Utah! Can you believe it? What's in . . ."

"If my dad tried to move me to Utah, I'd—"

Elizabeth and I looked at each other and started walking a little faster. Suddenly all I wanted to do was hide in a bathroom stall until the bell rang.

"Hey, guys! Really sorry to hear about the move," Bethel's semiboyfriend, Jameel, said as he walked by.

"Uh . . . thanks," I muttered, clutching my books. The skirt was such a bad choice. I couldn't even get a long stride going in this thing.

"A Wakefieldless junior high?" Richard Griggs said with a smirk when we passed his locker. He put his hand over his heart. "How will we survive?"

"Shut up, Richard," Elizabeth said. I almost smiled. That was so not Elizabeth.

A scrawny girl with red hair came up to us and grabbed us both in an oddly strong bear hug. When she pulled away, she looked us both in the eyes. "This place won't be the same without you," she said sincerely. Then she shook her head mournfully before walking off.

I grabbed Elizabeth's arm. "Who was that?" I asked her under my breath.

"I have no idea," she answered. Without another word we practically ran for our lockers. Unfortunately, that was the worst place we could possibly be. Almost everyone we knew was gathered in the hall between my locker and Elizabeth's. The second Kristin saw me and Elizabeth, she broke away from the crowd and came running over to meet us.

"How're you guys doing?" she asked, her brows knit in concern.

"What happened?" Elizabeth said in an uncharacteristically shrill voice. "Did someone announce the move over the PA system?"

Kristin grimaced and flushed, gazing down at the floor guiltily. That was when I realized what had really happened.

"Lacey," I said, narrowing my eyes.

"I'm sorry, guys," Kristin said, falling into step with us as we approached the group milling around our lockers. It looked like a funeral. "After Vito's yesterday, she got right on her cell phone and called everyone she knew," Kristin continued, eyeing me warily. "And I told Bethel. I thought she must know already, so I called her to talk, and I let it slip. I'm so sorry, Jess!"

There it was again. That feeling of heaviness throughout my body. "It's okay, Kristin," I responded, my shoulders sagging. "I'm sorry. I really wanted to tell you guys. I just thought I should tell Damon first, and it was so hard—"

"Hey, everyone," Elizabeth said, interrupting

me—and sounding so exhausted, you'd think the day was ending instead of just beginning. Eight more hours of this!

Bethel came over and put her arm around my shoulders. "What can I say except this stinks?" she said. I half smiled, then noticed Damon wasn't among the mourners. At least Bethel wasn't mad at me because she'd heard the news from someone else!

"Hey, Liz," Salvador said, maneuvering over to her on his crutches. She barely glanced at him. "You okay?"

"You know what? I'm fine!" Elizabeth snapped harshly. We all fell silent, and tension immediately filled the air. Elizabeth tucked her chin and fiddled with her backpack strap. "I'm sorry, I just don't want to talk about this anymore," she said. "Neither of us does. And everyone is talking about it. People we don't even know—"

She was going to cry. I could hear it in her voice. I put my hand on her arm. "Liz, it's okay. Come on, we'll just—"

I stopped midsentence when I saw Damon and Blue walking down the hall toward us. They glanced over, then did the classic, stare-straight-ahead-and-just-keep-walking thing. As if they didn't see us. As if anyone could miss the crowd of people standing there, watching Elizabeth and me as if we were aliens who'd just beamed into the middle of the hallway.

Elizabeth caught my eye. "What is that, the We Hate the Wakefields Club?"

I couldn't have said it better myself. It was so obvious what they were doing. They had probably complained about us all night and now figured they'd bonded over it or something. I couldn't take this anymore! Damon wasn't remotely acting like himself. He was acting like a total jerk. He was acting like—

"Oh, look! It's the soon-to-be Utah sisters! Howdy, cowgirls!"

Lacey Frells had really bad timing. And did they even have cows in Utah?

Elizabeth and I both whipped around to look at her. She was standing right behind us and, as always, had that awful smug look on her face.

"Hope you don't mind I told a few friends about your move," she said, tossing back her brown hair and smiling sarcastically.

My face must have turned bloodred because when I took a step toward Lacey, her smug smile vanished and she almost took a step back. I didn't even have the sense to be psyched about it. I was about to snap.

"You know what, Lacey?" I said, coming so close, we were practically nose to nose. "The one thing I'm not going to miss about this place is your hideous face, your pathetic fashion sense, and your awful, awful breath." She lifted her hand to cover her mouth, then realized what she'd done and pulled it away. "Oh, wait, that's three things, isn't it?" I said with a shrug. "My bad!"

Then I turned on my heel and stalked away so fast, no one could have even tried to stop me. So much for my positive attitude!

Salvador

After Jessica stormed off, I wanted to say something to wipe that depressed look off Elizabeth's face, but I felt totally awkward. What could I possibly say to make her feel better? She'd already bitten my head off once this morning. Still, I had to try. I couldn't take her feeling like this.

"Liz?" I said quietly. She turned slowly to look at me, her eyes all clouded. "Listen, it's going to be okay," I assured her. "In a few days everyone will be talking about someone else. I could still fall off my crutches in the middle of the cafeteria and rip my pants. The offer still stands."

"Works for me," Anna piped in.

The corners of Elizabeth's mouth twitched, and for a second I thought I had her. The good old del Valle humor had struck gold again. But then she sighed and took a step back. My stomach ached just to see her move away from me.

"I gotta go, you guys," she said, turning. "I'll see you later."

80

Then she walked off, without even a look back. I felt so bad for her, my whole body hurt. I leaned farther into my crutches, and my head sagged.

"She didn't mean to snap at you before, you know," Anna said, patting my back.

"Yeah, she's just stressed out," Bethel added. "With the move . . ."

"And Blue," Anna added.

Everyone started to head off to class, and Anna, Kristin, Bethel, and I made our way down the hall.

"I know," I said, watching my cast as it swung over the linoleum floor. "I just wish there was something we could do, you know? I mean, imagine if you were moving, and on top of it, everyone was fighting and stuff? They must be so depressed. I just wish Damon and Blue could chill out. How can we make everyone relax already?"

"Maybe there's a way," Anna said, stopping in her tracks so abruptly, Bethel, Kristin, and I were three steps ahead before we realized we should stop. All it took was one look at Anna's face for me to know exactly what she was thinking.

"A surprise party!" we said at the same time.

"Omigod! It's perfect!" Kristin exclaimed, looking at Bethel.

"I'm in," Bethel said, adjusting her backpack

on her shoulder. "Hey! I bet I could get my mom to cook. Jessica loves my mom's food."

"And the Doña can bake a cake . . . or ten," I said.

"I'll do decorations," Kristin put in. "I love that stuff."

"Well, we have some time to plan, right? I mean, it's not like they're moving tomorrow or anything."

"Yeah, but I think they need some serious cheering up, like, as soon as possible. It can be a you're-leaving-soon pick-me-up party," Bethel said. Anna and Kristin nodded.

At that moment the warning bell rang, and I looked around and realized the halls were practically empty. We started double-timing it off to class.

"Kristin, let's get together during study hall and make a list of things we need to do," Anna said as we rushed along.

"Who are we going to invite?" Bethel asked.

"That's easy," I said, concentrating on my crutches. I wasn't used to moving so fast. "Everyone."

"Everyone?" Anna said skeptically. I looked up at her, and I tripped myself, stumbling forward a few feet, then righting myself clumsily by leaning on one crutch.

"Don't challenge me when I'm trying to walk!" I said with a laugh.

"Sorry," Anna answered, reaching over to straighten my backpack, which was hanging off one shoulder. "I just meant . . . is Blue part of everyone?"

I pulled myself up as straight as possible and rolled back my shoulders. "I think it's about time Blue and I had a little talk," I said. "Man to man."

Blue

I looked at my new waterproof watch on Tuesday morning and rolled my eyes. I couldn't believe it was only nine o'clock and it was only Tuesday. This had already been the longest week in recorded history. I'd spent so much time thinking about Elizabeth, Elizabeth and Salvador, how to avoid Elizabeth and Salvador, I felt like I'd already put in five days at school. I couldn't wait to get out that afternoon and hit the surf.

I slammed my locker shut, tucked my math book under my arm, and turned to head off to class. I stopped in my tracks when I saw Salvador limping his way over to me, looking me right in the eye. I felt my adrenaline start to pump. I'd never hit a guy on crutches. Heck, I'd never hit a guy at all. But he was the last person I wanted to talk to.

"Hey, man," Salvador said as he came to a stop in front of me.

I didn't say anything.

"Okay," Salvador said. "Look, I know you're mad. And I want to talk to you about this whole Liz thing. I wanted to say I'm sorry for how things went down."

Right. I was so sure. He got Elizabeth. How could he be sorry about that?

Salvador eyed me, obviously thinking I was loopy since I wasn't talking. But I wasn't about to start blabbing just to make him feel more comfortable. Especially not after what he'd done.

"I swear I didn't mean to do anything to . . . you know . . . hurt your feelings," Salvador continued. "It just happened. I don't know what else to say except I'm sorry."

I watched Salvador for a second, and he just held my gaze. His face was totally open and sincere, and I felt myself start to loosen up. Just a little. The guy was genuinely sorry.

"All right," I said finally, feeling my balled fists unball. "I accept your apology."

Salvador nodded and smiled. "Thanks, man."

"But I want to know what this is really all about," I said, crossing my arms over my chest along with my math book. "Why do you care so much about how I feel?"

"Well, for one thing, you're my friend," Salvador said, leaning back against the lockers. "And when they do a *Behind the Music* on Big

85

Noise, I don't want a fight over a girl to be the thing that broke us up."

I chuckled against my will.

"But seriously, some of us were thinking of throwing a surprise party for Liz and Jessica, and I wanted to know if you'd come," Salvador said.

Oh. There it was.

"I don't think that's a good idea," I said, leaning back with him. We both stared at our reflections in the trophy case across the hall.

"How come?" Salvador asked.

"I'm not exactly in a party mood with everything that's been going on," I said with a shrug. "And I'm sure Damon's going to tell you the same thing. Who needs that kind of baggage at a going-away party?"

Salvador pushed himself away from the wall and leaned into his crutches, turning to look at me. "But that's exactly why I think you should come," he said. "To get rid of the baggage. That way everyone gets to say good-bye baggage free."

He did have a point. Did I really want Elizabeth to leave Sweet Valley forever hating me? Then again, did I really want to spend an entire night watching Elizabeth and Salvador kissing and looking into each other's eyes?

"I gotta go, man," I said, my face heating up

again. I had to get out of there before I had the urge to pummel the guy again. "Later," I said, starting off.

"Just think about it," Salvador called as I walked by.

I didn't say anything. All I wanted to do at that moment was get as far away from Salvador as possible.

Anna and Kristin's Party Plans

<u>To Do:</u>

1. Ask Mrs. Wakefield if we can have it at their house. (Kristin will call.)
2. Figure out a way to get the twins out of the house.
3. Food: Bethel's mom–BBQ chicken, salads
   Doña–desserts
   Kristin–veggies and dip
   Anna–Anna's famous chocolate-covered cornflakes
   Sal–drinks
   Larissa and Toby–junk food
4. Decorations: Streamers, balloons, bon voyage banner, plates, cups, forks, knives, etc.
5. Music: Get everyone to bring CDs and write their names on them.
6. Invites: E-mail invitations–Ask Ronald to design something cool on his computer.

<u>Guests:</u>
   Anna
   Kristin

Sal
Bethel
Damon
Blue
Brian
Toby
Larissa
Ronald
Bianca
Robby
Stacey
Sheryl
Chris
Lila?
Lacey???
Steven's friends?

Note to self: Finish this later. I have to study for Spanish!

Salvador

After second period I was making my way to the bathroom when Anna came running up to me.

"There you are! I've been looking all over for you!" she said, slightly out of breath.

"Well, I'm not that hard to find with these things," I joked, lifting one crutch.

Anna smiled and squeezed my arm. "This is serious," she said, leveling me with a stare. "You have to be really careful around Elizabeth."

"All righty," I said, giving her a skeptical look. "Is she wired with explosives or something?"

"No, stupid," Anna said. "I mean, you have to be really careful not to spill about the party."

"Oh," I said, my face flushing. "And you felt the need to tell me that because . . . ?"

Anna rolled her eyes and took a step back. "Do I have to remind you that you're the worst secret keeper on the face of the earth?"

"Hey!" I said, offended. "I'm not that ba—"

She put up her hand to silence me. "When I

90

had a crush on Matt Viola in fifth grade, who told him?"

"I did," I said matter-of-factly. "But he's bigger than me, and he really wanted to know."

She ignored my joke, obviously not in the mood. "And when we were having a surprise birthday bash for Sheryl Sacks in sixth grade, who asked her what she was wearing to the party?"

"I did," I answered again, hanging my head.

"And when we found out Chris Grassi's mom was pregnant and he specifically asked us not to tell anyone?" she prompted.

"I asked him if it was a boy or a girl in the middle of biology class," I muttered, feeling defeated.

"Should I go on?" Anna asked, raising one eyebrow. I was going to have to ask her to teach me how to do that one day. "Because there's more."

"No, you don't need to go on," I said, taking a deep breath. "I'll be careful around Liz."

She didn't seem convinced.

"I swear!" I said. I held up my right hand like I was taking an oath. "She is not going to find out about this party from me. No way. Nohow."

"Okay," Anna said. "Because this party has to be perfect."

"I know. I'll be good," I said. Of course, I

hadn't meant to spill any of those other secrets either. I always had good intentions. I was just a moron when it came to these things.

Suddenly I found myself worrying that it might be physically impossible for me to keep my mouth zippered shut for a few days.

Elizabeth

"Feeling better?" Jessica asked me as we paid for our lunches on Tuesday afternoon. I folded up my change and stuffed it into the small pocket of my backpack.

"Yeah, but I hope no one ever asks me if I'm okay again . . . for the rest of my life," I answered, picking up my tray. "I'm serious. I don't care if my eyeball is hanging out of its socket—I don't want anyone to ever ask me if I'm okay."

"Tell me about it," Jessica said as she followed me out into the cafeteria. "And Ronald went on for about fifteen minutes about how much he's going to miss having me as his locker partner. By the end of it I was consoling him!"

I laughed, which sounded really odd considering how little I'd been laughing lately. "Let's just promise we won't ever talk about it at lunch, or I won't be able to digest, okay?"

"Deal," Jessica said with a nod. She even managed a smile, and I was proud of her. I knew she was having a worse day than I was, what with the whole Damon thing going on. I bet she was walking through the halls, nervous that she might see him at any minute and wondering how he was going to act. I hated that feeling. Luckily I didn't see Damon anywhere in the cafeteria. Maybe he'd decided to eat in the library or something.

I approached the table, where I was surprised to see Salvador, Anna, Kristin, Brian, Bethel, Toby, and Larissa all sitting together, talking about something pretty intensely. Usually my and Jessica's friends are scattered all over the cafeteria at different tables. Plus the school is usually divided into two different lunches—but every once in a while both lunches are combined because of meetings or pep rallies or whatever. Today was one of those days.

"What are they doing?" I asked Jessica, pausing a few feet from the table.

"Search me," Jessica said with a shrug. She slid into a seat next to Bethel and plunked down her tray. No one even noticed. "Hi, guys!" Jessica called out loudly as I sat down next to Salvador.

Their heads all popped up, and the notebook they were looking at instantly disappeared into Kristin's backpack. Anna was doing something in her bag under the table, and Toby shoved half his burger into his mouth. Then Larissa leaned forward on the table, resting her head on her hand and effectively blocking out Anna and Kristin.

"I haven't had a chance to tell you girls how much I'm going to miss you!" Larissa said dramatically. But then, she said almost everything dramatically.

"Thanks," I said, shooting Salvador a confused look. He was hunched over his tray, continually shoving french fries into his mouth like he was chain eating. My stomach turned. Maybe he was trying not to look at me because I had snapped at him earlier. He hadn't even acknowledged me yet. "Hungry, Sal?" I joked, hoping to break the ice.

"Mmmm," he answered, his mouth full. He grabbed his soda, took a long drink through his straw, and went back to his fries.

I glanced around the table, and everyone seemed to be acting normally again. Jessica and Bethel were deep in conversation, and everyone else was talking about something silly Ronald had done in gym class. Now was my chance to apologize to Salvador.

"Listen, about this morning," I began, eyeing Salvador's profile. He kept eating. "I'm really sorry about the way that I snapped at you. I was just really tense, you know?"

Elizabeth

Salvador nodded a few times, giving me a quick glance out of the corner of his eye as he took another swig of soda. He swallowed hard— he probably had about fifty crunched-up fries in his mouth—and finally turned to look at me.

"It's fine," he said quickly. "Don't worry about it."

"You're sure?" I said, unconvinced. He was acting so weird. Weird for Salvador, even.

"Yeah, yeah, I'm sure," he said. "Everything's—"

"So, what's going on this weekend?" Jessica asked, addressing the whole group.

I saw Salvador's eyes widen a bit, and he jumped up, grabbing his backpack off the back of his chair. "I have to go," he said. He looked left and right, standing on his good leg. His crutches were leaning on the end of the table next to me.

"Could you pull in?" he asked me.

"Yeah, sure," I said, pulling my chair as close to the table as possible. I looked up at him as he hobbled behind me and grabbed his crutches. "Do you need help?" I asked.

"No!" he blurted out. Everyone looked up at him. Why was he acting so nuts? "I just . . . I have to go."

"Okay," I said. I glanced over at Jessica, and she raised her eyebrows as if to say, "You're the one who likes the freak."

Salvador took off, swinging his way along the side of the cafeteria where there wasn't so much traffic. I just sat there and watched him, feeling like I'd been slapped in the face. What had just happened here?

"He . . . uh . . . probably just needed to go to the bathroom," Anna said, filling the awkward silence with a chuckle.

Conversation started up around me again, but I just slumped back in my chair, looking at Salvador's half-eaten burger and half-finished soda. He never left until his plate was empty and usually went for seconds. Something was wrong. Maybe he was still mad at me for losing my temper earlier. I sighed and picked at my food. Anna might be right. He might have just headed for the bathroom. But I had a sneaking suspicion that all he'd wanted to do was get away from me.

Jessica

"Okay, is it just me, or are all our friends acting like total loonies?" I said as Elizabeth and I headed down the main hall after lunch. I was scanning the halls for Damon and trying hard not to look like I was scanning the halls for Damon. I'd checked my hair and makeup before we left the caf, and I looked great. If he saw me now, he would be eating his heart out in no time.

"Thank you!" Elizabeth said, throwing up her hands. "I thought it was just me. What was with that twenty-minute-long conversation about the weather?"

"I know! Like the weather in Sweet Valley ever changes," I said. Did I sound normal? I thought I did. Even though we were coming up on the hall where Damon's locker was and he always went to his locker after lunch.

"I wonder what the weather's like in Utah," Elizabeth said, looking off into nowhere.

I stopped and glared at her. "Bring me down, why don't you?"

"Sorry," she said, snapping out of it. "I'll see you later."

Before I could beg her not to leave me alone, she'd disappeared into the crowded hallway, heading off for her English class. I was on my own.

"Just hold your head high, don't look toward his locker, and don't panic," I muttered under my breath. Of course, the second I turned the corner, my eyes darted right to his locker, and there he was, looking perfect as always. He didn't even have the decency to look tired from a sleepless night trying to figure out how to win me back. He was just standing there in a black T-shirt and jeans, running his hand through his thick brown hair and looking at a notebook as if his world wasn't totally askew. What a jerk.

Should I go over there and talk to him? I thought as dozens of kids shoved by me, probably wondering why I was standing in the middle of the hall, looking dazed. Maybe I should just go over there and talk to him. But then again, why should I go up to him? He was the one who had acted like a jerk. He was the one who hadn't apologized or called or even tried to talk to me since Monday. Why should I be the one to—

My indignant train of thought hit the emergency brakes when I saw Blue walk up to

Damon. They immediately fell into some kind of intense conversation, and neither of them even noticed me standing there like a moron—thank God.

Suddenly I stopped feeling uncertain and started getting angry. What was with these two? What were they doing over there—plotting against me and Elizabeth? How immature could you be?

Finally I snapped out of it, turned on my heel, and stalked away before either one of them could spot me. The last thing I wanted was for Blue and Damon to think that Elizabeth and I actually cared about them.

Wednesday

8:45 A.M. The twins arrive at school and head for their lockers, only to find that no one is waiting there for them—except Ronald, who is wistfully staring at Jessica's books.

9:11 A.M. After the homeroom bell rings, Anna and Kristin meet up in the stairwell to discuss decorations. Kristin informs Anna she's going with a rainbow color scheme to be as cheerful as possible. Anna checks off her list until she gets to plates, which Kristin forgot to buy. Anna says she'll take care of it. Then Jessica walks in, and Kristin grabs her and drags her off to class while Anna hides her notes.

9:55 A.M. After history class Elizabeth tries to flag down Anna, but she tells Elizabeth she has to go get her books for study hall. Elizabeth tries to talk to Salvador instead, but he tells her he has to get to the nurse's office for some parentally approved painkillers. Elizabeth walks to her next class alone.

10:32 A.M. Jessica asks Bethel what she's doing on Friday, and Bethel tells her she's baby-sitting her little cousins. Jessica offers to help, but Bethel turns her down and bolts for class. Jessica's confused. They had so much fun the last time they baby-sat together. At least Jessica thought they did.

10:33 A.M. Bethel meets up with Anna in the stairwell, and Anna puts her on plate duty. Bethel salutes and heads for class. Anna makes another check in her notebook.

12:05 P.M. Jessica finds Kristin at lunch and asks her if she wants to do something on Friday. Kristin tells her she already made plans with Lacey. But Jessica's totally welcome to come if she . . . Jessica says thanks, but no thanks.

12:10 P.M. Anna finds Kristin and asks her if she called Jessica's old friend Lila yet. Kristin slaps her hand to her forehead, borrows Lacey's cell phone, and leaves a message on Lila's machine, laying out the details and apologizing for the short notice. When she hands the phone back to Lacey, Lacey asks her what time she should be there. Anna and Kristin share a wary glance. Guess Lacey's invited.

3:00 P.M. Elizabeth shuffles to her locker and finds Jessica there alone. They give each other miserable looks, put their arms around each other, and sulk their way to the front door. Yesterday everyone was upset that they were leaving, but now no one seems to care. Maybe they won't miss SVJH so much after all. . . .

3:45 P.M. Jessica calls Lila and asks her what she's doing on Friday. Lila tells her she's doing her nails. Jessica hangs up on her.

5:05 P.M. Elizabeth and Jessica stare at the phone, which hasn't rung once all afternoon. Apparently their so-called friends think they've already moved.

Damon

When I got to Blue's house on Thursday evening, I expected to hear the guys practicing already. As usual I was running late, and normally they were halfway through a song and ready to get on my back the second I got there. But instead of the wail of Brian's sax and the crash of Blue's drums, the place was eerily quiet.

"Hey, man." Blue popped up from behind his drum set when I stepped into the garage. I almost jumped back.

"Trying to give me a heart attack?" I asked, putting my guitar case down on the floor. I popped it open and pulled out my guitar, flinging the strap around my neck. "Where is everybody?"

"Not coming," Blue said, smashing a cymbal as I stood up. "I tried to call you, but you had already left." He pounded out a few halfhearted beats on his drums, then grabbed the cymbal to stop it from clanging.

"You're kidding," I said, looking around at the

mikes Salvador and Brian usually occupied. I strummed my guitar and tuned it.

"This is my serious face," Blue said, pointing to his chin with a drumstick. "They're over at Kristin's house, planning the big Wakefield bon voyage extravaganza." There was more than a little bit of bitterness in his voice.

I plopped down on a stool, resting my guitar in my lap, and let out a frustrated sigh. "Unbelievable. Jessica and I break up just when all of our friends start talking about nothing but the Wakefields."

"I know the feeling, man," Blue said. He started tossing his drumstick up and down distractedly. "It's, like, all Wakefields, all the time."

"Seriously," I added. "No one even cares that they totally dissed us."

Blue sucked in a long breath, then tipped back his head, staring up at the rafters in the perfectly clean garage. "I guess it's more important to them that Liz and Jessica are moving than it is that we had our hearts brutally mashed."

"Yeah, I guess," I said, my shoulders slumping. "So far, this week has reeked."

"Well, at least you have options, my man," Blue said, thumping the bass drum methodically. "At least you could have Jessica if you wanted her."

My heart squeezed painfully. Could I? After

the argument we'd had, I wasn't so sure. Would she let me apologize if I tried to? Knowing Jessica's stubbornness, my guess was no. And besides, I was still mad at her. The fact that I missed her didn't change the fact that she'd made me feel like an idiot.

"What're you thinking?" Blue asked me.

I glanced over at him, looking as pathetic as I felt, all hunched over behind his drums.

"I don't know," I said honestly. I strummed my guitar once, and the sound reverberated through the silent garage.

"Well, I'm thinking I'd rather have Elizabeth as a friend than not have her around at all," Blue said.

"But soon she's not going to be around . . . at all," I reminded him, my heart flopping again as I was reminded of Jessica's approaching departure.

"That's my point," Blue said, his voice sounding more sure of itself. "I mean, if Liz were going to be around forever, I could do the slow-torture routine—you know, drag out the guilt. But . . . well . . . don't you want to make the most of the time you have left with Jessica?"

I hung my head. The guy had a point. This might be one of those things that would probably go away after a week or two of dodging the subject and not quite talking about it. But we didn't have a lot of time to mess with. "So what do we do?" I said. "I don't even know if Jessica will talk to me."

Blue sighed and looked around the garage as if the tool-covered walls were going to have some answer for us. Then his eyes rested on Salvador's microphone, and he slowly smiled.

"I think I have an idea. . . ."

Elizabetn

"Liz, are you okay?" Jessica asked me as we quickly walked through the halls on Friday morning. The second the question was past her lips, I stopped in my tracks and glared at her.

"Didn't I say I never wanted anyone to ask me that again?" I said, crossing my arms.

Jessica's face flushed. "Sorry, master," she said sarcastically. "What's your deal? Why are you suddenly acting like a marine?"

"Look, I have something to do, and I just want to get it over with," I said, spinning on my heel and almost whacking her in the face with my flying ponytail. I was going to go up to Salvador and make him talk to me. This was ridiculous. We hadn't really talked since the little incident on Tuesday morning. Tuesday! That was three whole days ago! I wanted to spend as much time with Salvador as possible before we left, but he hadn't even called me yesterday or the day before. And it was pretty obvious he'd been avoiding me at school. He was either still mad at me for yelling at him, which I had totally apologized for, or he'd suddenly decided he didn't want to be with me anymore. Either way, I was determined to find out what was going on.

When I turned the corner to go to my locker, Salvador, Anna, and Kristin were all hanging out, chatting. I walked right up to them, Jessica at my heels, half expecting them to all make excuses to walk away just like they had all day yesterday.

"Hi, guys!" I said, faking cheer. "What's going on?"

"Not much," Anna said with a shrug and a smile. "What's going on with you?"

"Nothing," I said. I glanced up at Salvador, who was just standing there, or leaning on his crutches, actually, appearing totally innocent. "Hi!" I said, looking him directly in the eye.

"Hi," he returned, flashing a brilliant smile. "You look really . . . nice."

Anna rolled her eyes, Kristin giggled, and I just stood there with my mouth open. What the heck was going on around here? Was he really acting like nothing had happened?

"Uh . . . thanks," I said, smiling back and blushing like crazy. I guess he'd finally forgiven me. Maybe I'd just imagined the silent-treatment stuff. Maybe every time I tried to talk to him, he really had had somewhere else to be. He limped around Kristin to stand beside me, and I pulled him over a few feet, away from the others. At first

Elizabeth

I was going to ask him if everything was really okay between the two of us, but I decided to let it slide. What was the point in going over it all again? Time, after all, was precious at this point.

"So, do you have plans for tonight?" I asked, smiling up at him.

His face immediately lost all its color. "Uh . . . kind of?" he said, glancing over his shoulder.

My heart fell. "Oh . . . really?" I said. "Because I . . . I was kind of hoping we could—"

"Well, I don't really have plans, exactly," he said quickly. "I don't mean to say there's any kind of plan because it's not like there's anything big going on. Not at all. I just, I'm—"

I was starting to feel like he was avoiding the issue here. "Sal," I said. "If you don't want to go out with me tonight, just say so."

At that moment Anna's hand came down on Salvador's shoulder, and we both turned to look at her. "Sal, don't you have to go get that math homework we were going to go over?" she asked, looking at him pointedly.

"Yes!" he said, very loudly. I could have sworn he was sweating. "Yes, I do. Thank you! For . . . reminding me." He started to make his way off and then, as an afterthought, glanced back at me. "Later, Liz."

And with that, he took off as fast as his little crutches could carry him.

Salvador

"Sal!" Elizabeth called after me as I crutched my way down the hall at warp speed. Or warp speed for crutches, which is about the speed at which the Doña window-shops.

I had almost slipped back there. I really had. I'm that pathetic when it comes to thinking before I speak. It generally doesn't happen. That was why my mouth had gotten me into so much trouble over the years. As a kid, I'd tasted more soap than cookies. And there were always a lot of cookies in my house.

"Sal!" She was getting closer. I got tired of acting deaf and stopped to let her catch up. Man, I couldn't wait until we yelled "surprise" that night. Then maybe I could relax.

Okay, just play it cool, I told myself. *You won't spill. You won't. Just say as little as possible.*

I turned to look into Elizabeth's beautiful blue-green eyes, and they were practically bulging out of her head. This girl was mad. My palms started to sweat so much, they slipped around on the grips of my crutches. *Play it cool.* . . .

"Liz, is something wrong?" I asked, legitimately concerned.

"Yeah, something's wrong," she spat back sarcastically, placing her hands on her little hips. "Like the fact that you can't seem to forgive me for one tiny outburst!"

Forgive her? What the heck was she talking about?

"Liz, I—"

"God, Sal, how could you be so insensitive?" she blurted out. She noticed that people were watching her, amused, as they walked by, and lowered her voice a notch. "You know how upset I am about this move, and you know it has nothing to do with you. Plus I apologized!"

I was still completely clueless as to what she was talking about, and it must have shown on my face.

"Great, and now you're playing dumb?" Elizabeth said. "You're going to try to tell me that you haven't been giving me the silent treatment for days?"

Oh! Finally it dawned on me. I'd been avoiding her because I didn't want to spill about the party, and she thought I was mad at her for snapping at me—something so insignificant, I'd completely forgotten about it.

"I haven't been giving you the silent treatment because I was mad at you," I said, trying to reassure her with a nice steady look into her eyes. Meanwhile my heart was pounding. *Don't say anything else,* I told myself. *Don't even hint at anything else.*

She stood up straight, looking a little bit relieved but still confused. "Why, then?" she asked. "Why did you avoid me since I yelled at you and then not even call me for the past couple of nights?"

I felt my face turn bright red and glanced around, hoping Anna would be there to save me again. She was nowhere to be found. I had no excuse for this. I racked my brain but came up with nothing. "I was just really . . . busy," I muttered finally.

Elizabeth's face went hard, as if someone had just turned her to cement. Uh-oh.

"You know what, Sal? If you don't want to talk to me . . . then maybe . . . maybe this whole thing was a mistake to begin with," Elizabeth said, her voice cracking on the word *whole.*

I felt like someone had just kicked me in the gut. "This whole thing?" I said. She didn't mean—

"Yeah!" Elizabeth blurted out. "Maybe I never should have kissed you in the first place!"

Then, before my thick head could even process what was happening, she turned and stalked off.

Elizabeth's Journal

my friends are total jerks. I can't believe the way they're acting. The guys have suddenly become completely heartless, and the girls . . . normally everyone hangs out on friday night. we usually have too many things to do. But now that we're leaving, it's like everyone's too busy to hang out with Jessica and me. what is it? They figure we're moving, so why be bothered? I really can't believe this.

I guess we shouldn't have been so worried about breaking our bad news. no one really cares anyway.

Jessica

By the time Elizabeth and I got home from school on Friday, the sky was clouding over to match our moods. Apparently the only person in all of Sweet Valley that was sad to see us go was Mother Nature. Elizabeth opened the door for me without a word, and I kind of clomped my way into the house, my shoulders sagging, my feet heavy, and premature frown lines definitely forming on my forehead. I dropped my bag at the bottom of the stairs, Elizabeth did the same, and we tromped our way into the kitchen.

We both knew what we were going for without saying a thing. Ice cream. Lots of it.

I pushed open the swinging door into the kitchen and wasn't at all surprised to see Steven already sitting at the table. His head was propped up on one hand, and he was slowly lifting a spoonful of Rocky Road to his mouth, the open carton of ice cream in front of him, with drips melting down the side and onto the table.

Jessica

He looked up at us and pushed two spoons across the tile table in our direction. "I got them out just in case," he said.

Elizabeth and I pulled up two chairs as close to the carton as possible and joined our brother. Maybe this move wouldn't be so bad after all. No one seemed to want us here, and at least we had each other.

"I can't believe how low we've sunk," Elizabeth said, gazing at a heaping spoonful of ice cream.

"Tell me about it," Steven added.

"We're not even fighting," I said.

Steven sighed and licked his spoon. "Never thought I'd see the day."

"Life stinks," Elizabeth said.

We nodded in agreement. At the beginning of the year I'd thought I could never be more depressed than I was about switching schools and leaving all my friends behind. I had no idea what I was talking about.

Just as we all lifted another spoonful to our mouths, we heard the front door close, and moments later our mom walked into the kitchen. She took one look at us and froze, grocery bags in her arms, keys dangling from one finger.

"What are you kids doing?" she asked. No one answered. She dropped her stuff, walked over, and took the ice cream away. We didn't even blink. "Who are you, and what have you done with my children?" she asked, raising her eyebrows.

We slumped in our chairs.

"Okay!" she said, slapping the lid on the ice cream and grabbing the spoons out of our hands one by one. She tossed them in the sink, put the ice cream in the freezer, and picked up her keys again. "We're getting out of this house. It's time to shake off all this negativity."

She earned three simultaneous eye rolls with that one.

"C'mon, guys," she prodded. "Your father's working late. . . . Why don't we go get some pizza? Have a little fun?"

"Sure," Elizabeth said sarcastically.

"Fine," I grumbled.

"Whatever," Steven said tonelessly.

Yeah. This was going to be a great time!

Elizabeth

Sitting at Vito's with most of my family, I was so tense, I couldn't even think about eating. I just knew that at any moment Salvador and Anna and Larissa and Toby and who knew who else were going to walk in together, ready to chow down and have some fun with their new, smaller group of friends. How stupid did they think we were? Didn't they realize how obvious it was that they were avoiding me and Jessica? I pulled a napkin out of the dispenser on the table and started ripping it into little shreds.

"Cathy has been totally moody ever since I told her," Steven told my mom as he twirled his straw in his soda. "It's like, one second she's holding on to me like I'm going off to war, and the next second she's ignoring me."

"She's going to miss you, Steven," my mother said in a soothing voice. "She doesn't know how to deal with it, that's all."

Steven let out a huff of air. "Could've fooled

me," he said. "If she's going to miss me so much, why does she keep flirting with Tom Szwarsky?"

"Because she's a girl," my mom said.

"Hey!" Jessica and I both blurted out, offended. Then we looked at each other, and we all laughed.

"I'm glad Damon's not doing that," Jessica said. "The silent treatment is bad enough. If he started flirting with Lacey or something, I think I'd die."

"That's not going to happen," I told her. "Damon is totally gaga over you."

"Yeah, so why is he ignoring me?" Jessica asked, brushing her hair back from her face.

"Because he's a guy," my mom said with a smile.

"Hey!" Steven protested in a high-pitched voice.

We all laughed again, and I felt myself slowly starting to relax. It was nice to see my family smile again.

"Give it a little time," my mom said as the steaming-hot pizza was placed down on our table. "Everyone will cool off and realize what's important."

"Ya think?" I asked, still wondering what had gone wrong with Salvador.

"I know," my mom said, looking us each in

the eye. "People can surprise you. And in the meantime we have pizza to devour."

Everyone pushed aside their sodas and dug in. Suddenly I felt like I hadn't eaten in days. Maybe Mom was right. I'd take the weekend to chill and take a break from my friends. By the time Monday rolled around, maybe everything would be better. And if not, I'd deal with it. It was time to stop moping, and when I looked at Jessica and Steven, I could tell that they were feeling better too. We were going to get through this move thing, friends or no friends.

Salvador

I was so nervous standing in the foyer at the Wakefields' on Friday night, I felt like I was going to shake apart. My heart was going on overdrive, but I was trying to look calm. After all, I had an important job to fulfill here. I, Salvador del Valle, was the signal giver.

How I had been nominated for this position, I would never understand.

I pulled the sheer white curtain aside from the window again and peeked out. I was supposed to let everyone know when Mrs. Wakefield's car pulled onto the street. Sounds easy enough, but there was one tiny, unforeseen problem. Every single car looks alike in the pitch freakin' dark!

Suddenly a pair of headlights turned onto the block, and I saw a flash on the side of the car, thanks to a particularly bright streetlight. It was blue, and it looked long. It had to be the Wakefields' minivan.

"They're here!" I shouted into the crowded living room.

"Shhh!" was the response from the thirty or so people gathered there.

I scowled. "They're not outside the door— they're pulling into the driveway!" I whispered hoarsely.

"Get out back!" Anna whispered. I narrowed my eyes at her. She looked good in her little red dress, but the look she gave me back was pure evil.

"Okay! I'm going!" I said. Every pore in my body was producing sweat as I made my way through the dark house. I stepped over Kristin, who was lying under the coffee table with her feet sticking out. Then I shook my head in disbelief when I saw Ronald standing in the corner with a lampshade balanced on his head. Toby, Larissa, and Bianca, their friends from drama, were hud- dled behind the couch, giggling, and Lacey rolled her eyes at me from her position against the wall, behind a standing plant. Anna's mom and my grandmother headed into the den, where they'd stashed the massive cake the Doña had baked. Then I saw the most unbelievable thing I'd seen yet—Bethel McCoy and Jessica's old friend Lila, ducking into a closet to hide with Bethel's boyfriend, Jameel, and Chris Grassi. If you'd asked me yesterday, I would have said Bethel and Lila wouldn't even come near each other at this party. But I guess anything could happen.

Steven's girlfriend, Cathy, was hanging out with some of Jessica's track friends in the kitchen, and I told them to hide as I made my way through to the backyard, where the rest of our band, Big Noise, was waiting.

I felt a chill the second I joined them, even though the night was seriously warm. Blue was still acting less than comfortable around me, and Damon seemed to be following his lead. I wondered if we'd all be talking by the end of the night. I hoped so.

"They're coming," I told them, grabbing my microphone and fiddling with the stand so I wouldn't have to look anyone in the eye.

Then I felt someone step up to me, and my heart raced even faster. If I kept this up, I was going to be the youngest ever coronary patient at Fowler Memorial Hospital.

"Hey," I said flatly, looking into Blue's expressionless eyes.

"Hey. I just wanted to tell you this is a cool thing you did," Blue said. He looked at me for a second and then extended his hand. I smiled and shook it.

"Thanks," I said, looking around at Damon and Brian. "But it's a good thing we're all doing, right?"

"Yeah," Brian said with a smile. Damon nodded distractedly.

"So, we're all cool?" I asked, feeling a huge weight lift off my shoulders.

"We're cool," Damon answered. Blue clapped me on the shoulder and headed for the stool behind his drum set.

Damon cleared his throat. "So . . . let's do this," he said, strumming his guitar.

I reached up and straightened my microphone, glad to be past the uncomfortable part. Now all I had to do was make sure everything was okay between me and Elizabeth.

Jessica

By the time we got home from Vito's, I was in a much better mood, but I was totally ready to pass out. It had been a long, long week, and all I could think about was getting under the covers, sleeping late in the morning, and then figuring out what to do about Damon.

Steven led the way up the front steps and was about to open the door when my mother put her hand on his upper arm.

"Ladies first, Steven," she said, letting Elizabeth and me walk ahead of him. I shot Elizabeth a look, like where did *that* come from? My mother was big on manners, but I'd never heard her harp on that particular one.

Elizabeth shrugged, pulled out her keys, and opened the door. Together we walked through the darkened foyer and into the living room.

"Surprise!"

My heart flew into my throat as all the lights blazed on and about a million voices cheered all around me. When I started breathing again, I looked at Elizabeth's shocked face and laughed. There were camera flashes going off from every direction, causing little colored squares to blur my vision, but I could tell that just about everyone we knew was standing in our living room, laughing and clapping. There was a rainbow of streamers draped all over the place and balloons covered the floor and ceiling. A banner hung on the far wall read, We'll Miss You, Elizabeth and Jessica!

Suddenly Kristin came up and hugged me hard. "Are you surprised?" she asked gleefully, clicking her camera right in my face.

"Are you kidding me?" I asked, glancing over at Elizabeth, who was hugging Anna. "I can't believe you guys did this!" I was laughing as I spoke—it seemed like I couldn't stop myself. This was why everyone had been acting so weird for the past few days! They hadn't forgotten about us already.

"We're gonna miss you, Wakefield," Bethel said, coming up and giving me a quick hug.

"I'm going to miss you too," I said. As I looked past her shoulder, I saw Lila Fowler walking over, her eyes shimmering with tears.

"Hey, Jess," she said.

"I can't believe you're here!" I exclaimed, hugging her next. Wow. Our friends had done an amazing job. I had never felt more . . . special in my entire life. Everyone who cared about us had shown up to let us know.

I scanned the crowded room of friendly faces, looking for one in particular but not finding it. Surely Damon had been invited. Was it possible he'd just decided not to show?

Elizabeth

"You had no idea, did you?" Larissa asked me as I stood at the doorway to the living room, still shocked so badly, I couldn't even move.

"None," I said, thinking back to how depressed Jessica and I had been when we'd gotten home from school that afternoon. Our bags were still sitting where we'd dropped them, at the foot of the stairs, but the rest of the house was like a completely different place. I'd never seen more balloons in my life. Even Anna's and Bethel's moms were there, and Steven was in the corner, hugging his girlfriend, who was grinning from ear to ear. I couldn't have stopped smiling if I'd tried.

Just then Salvador's grandma walked in holding a huge, beautiful cake. At the same time I heard an electric guitar wail, and everyone looked toward the back of the house. Out of nowhere loud music filled the air. What had they done—moved the stereo to the backyard? I looked at the entertainment system. Still intact. So where was the music coming from?

Just as Jessica and I glanced at each other in confusion, someone started singing, and my whole body tingled. Was that . . . ?

"Sal?" Jessica and I said in unison.

"C'mon!" Anna said, practically jumping up and down with excitement. She cleared a path through the crowd with me, Jessica, Larissa, Kristin, and Bethel following. "You are going to just die when you see this!" Anna called over her shoulder.

On our way through the house I saw so many familiar faces, and I couldn't believe they were all there for us. That afternoon I'd thought I had no friends. Boy, was I wrong!

We came out onto the patio, and my heart pretty much stopped beating. There was Salvador, looking like a full-on rock star, singing the words to our song, "Oreo Eyes," while Damon, Brian, and Blue . . . yes, Blue, backed him up on their instruments. Big Noise was playing our party! At that moment I couldn't have been more psyched if I'd found a world-famous platinum rock band in my backyard.

Salvador looked up, caught my eye, and smiled, and I nearly melted right there. As the song came to an end, he lifted his hand and waved. Jessica grabbed my hand and squeezed it, and I knew exactly what she was feeling—a mixture of excitement and nervousness. I knew she was worried about what would happen between her and Damon. But at least he was here. That had to mean something.

"I have a little speech to make now that the guests of honor are here," Salvador said into the microphone. People streamed through the sliding-glass doors and crowded onto the patio, even stretching out along the sides of the pool behind the band.

"We have all gathered here tonight to say good-bye to the Wakefield sisters . . . who we're all going to miss very much," Salvador said, looking directly into my eyes. I blushed so hard, I thought my skin was going to be permanently red. "But this night is not about how sad we're going to be without them," he continued, lowering his voice in mock seriousness. "It's about Elizabeth and Jessica. So ladies . . . this one's for you."

Blue lifted his drumsticks and slapped them together, counting out the beat. "One! Two! Three! Four!"

Then the band launched into a funky rendition of the old song "What I Like About You." Jessica and I both cracked up laughing as the crowd started to cheer and clap along with the music. A few people even started to dance as Salvador sang.

Anna grabbed me and twirled me around, and I dipped her, laughing the whole time. I couldn't have imagined a better end to an awful week. And the best thing about it was that Salvador and Blue and Damon all looked relaxed and happy. There didn't seem to be any tension in the air as they played. Maybe everything really was going to be okay.

Damon

The second we were done with the song, I put my guitar back in its stand and headed straight for Jessica. The crowd was cheering, but I barely even noticed. All I could think about was talking to Jessica and getting her to forgive me for acting like such a jerk.

I walked right up to her and grabbed her hand without saying a word. Luckily she didn't put up a fight. I had to find a quiet spot where we could talk before the whole party found its way back inside. The living room was practically empty right then, but Steven flicked on the stereo and cranked it up. The place would be a mob scene in seconds. I looked at Jessica, and she must have known what I was thinking.

"Dining room," she said.

"Right." We walked into the dining room, and she pulled me over to the far corner into the small space between the cabinet that held all the plates and a big, leafy plant. It was perfect. I looked down into her blue-as-the-ocean eyes, and my mouth went dry. Now if I could just figure out what to say.

"So . . . ," she said, wiping her hands on her black pants.

"I'm sorry," I blurted out. She blinked up at me as if she was surprised.

"Damon, I—"

"Wait. Let me finish before I forget everything," I said. I put my hands on her shoulders, and my knees actually weakened just from touching her. "I've been a total idiot," I said. "I was waiting for you to apologize again when I should have just . . . been there for you. So I'm sorry."

"It's okay," Jessica said, lifting my hands off her shoulders and holding them down in front of us. "I should have told you. I just felt like as long as you didn't know, it wouldn't feel real. I know it sounds stupid," she said, an embarrassed laugh escaping her lips.

"No. It doesn't," I said. I reached up and ran one finger along her perfect cheek. I couldn't believe she was leaving. Really, truly leaving. I felt totally empty and totally filled with emotions all at the same time. I ran my hand along her hair, and she smiled. "I'm going to miss you," I said.

"I'm going to miss you too," she answered, her voice cracking.

I looked her in the eyes and then leaned

down to kiss her. She reached up and held me tightly around the neck, and we kissed for a long time. Like if we stopped, we'd never get a chance to kiss again. Then she finally broke away and hugged me. I hugged her back, and it felt like nothing I'd ever felt before. I was totally relieved to have her in my arms again, but at the same time it was like I was afraid to let her go.

So I didn't. And we just stayed there, hugging, as the party started to rage in the other room.

Salvador

"I'm glad you're talking to me again," Elizabeth said as we sat on lounge chairs out by her pool. Most of the crowd had gone back inside, but Elizabeth had steered me over here when we were done with our song. It was funny. While we were singing, it was like everything was fine. I'd forgotten to be tense. Totally spaced on the fact that Elizabeth had publicly bawled me out that morning.

"I was never not talking to you!" I protested, sitting up quickly. I winced and moved my cast into a more comfortable position.

"You have been acting like a freak for the past few days, though," Elizabeth said with a laugh. She looked out over the sparkling pool water—the same color as her eyes. "I guess now I know why."

"I'm really bad at keeping secrets," I explained. "If I was acting weird, it was just because I was afraid of spilling the beans."

Elizabeth laughed again and shook her head. "I can't believe I didn't figure it out," she said, glancing over at me. "Now that I think about it, it's so obvious. All of you guys making notes together, clamming up the second we came by, giving us lame excuses for not hanging out . . ."

"Yeah, we're not exactly James Bonds," I said. I turned to face her, swinging my cast over so that it was resting on the patio. "Anna and Kristin and Bethel and I just wanted to show you guys how much we're going to miss you. And everyone pitched in. Having the band play was Damon and Blue's idea." Elizabeth's eyebrows rose when she heard that. I wasn't surprised that she was shocked to find out Blue had contributed. "That was the point," I told her. "We wanted to just do something that would make everyone . . . happy again."

At that moment there was a huge cheer from the living room—for what I had no idea—and Elizabeth and I both cracked up laughing.

"Well, it looks like it worked," Elizabeth said, standing up. She reached out both her hands, and I took them so she could pull me to my feet. She put her arms around my neck, lacing her fingers together lightly, and smiled. "Thanks," she said, her eyes gleaming. "Now, let's dance."

I looked down at my cast and shrugged. "We can try."

We made our way slowly into the house,

through the kitchen, and out into the living room, where we found out what everyone had been cheering about. Larissa and Ronald were in the middle of a big circle, dancing, and Ronald looked like he'd seen one too many boy-band videos. He was all over the place, but everyone was clapping along to the music and Larissa was laughing as she tried to keep up with him—and keep him from stepping all over her.

"You don't see that every day," Elizabeth said, pulling me over to the outskirts of the crowd. Everyone was starting to dance again, and Elizabeth started to move in front of me. Normally I'd probably be all over the dance floor, but my cast kept me from moving much.

I tried to move my arms, but I had to hold on to my crutches. I blushed and looked at Elizabeth, who just smiled encouragingly at me. Then I tried moving my good leg, and I started to fall over. Her eyes widened, and she reached out to steady me.

"Are you okay?" she asked with a laugh.

"Yeah, yeah," I said, standing up straight again. "I think I just figured out one move I can do," I told her.

She stepped back and put her hands on her hips. "Really? Let's see it," she said, looking me up and down.

"Okay, but it's pretty intense," I told her. "I don't want you to go crazy and throw yourself at me." She rolled her eyes, and with that, I started my new signature dance—bobbing my head up and down to the music. It was all I could do to keep a straight face, knowing how ridiculous I must look.

Elizabeth lasted two seconds before doubling over laughing, and all I had to do was take one look at her scrunched-up face and I cracked up myself. Once she got ahold of herself, she reached up and hugged me.

"This is the best thing anyone has ever done for me," she whispered in my ear.

I was so overwhelmed, for the first time in my life I couldn't say anything. So I just hugged her right back.

Jessica

Finally, after what seemed like forever, I broke away from Damon. I didn't really want to, but I knew we had to get back to the party. Sooner or later either Elizabeth or my mom was going to come looking for us, and I didn't want them to break in on our perfect moment. Not to mention the fact that my mom would burst about a million blood vessels if she caught Damon and me kissing and hugging in a secluded corner.

"So," I said, looking up into his eyes. "Wanna dance?"

"Definitely," he answered with a smile.

We slipped out of our hiding place and made our way back to the living room. The place looked like one of those raves they have in movies. The couches and table were pushed up against the walls. People were jumping up and down, batting balloons all over the place and making tons of noise. No one even noticed us as we hit the "dance floor."

Damon slapped hands with Brian Rainey, and we started to dance with him and Kristin. There's nothing better than dancing when you're looking for a tension release. It was just what I needed. Brian had never been comfortable with dancing, so he just basically jumped around, and I laughed when I saw Kristin trying to guard her feet from him. Damon was moving casually to the beat, and I wasn't even paying attention to my moves. I was just letting myself go. Everything was perfect. Well, as perfect as it could be.

The song ended, and a slow one started up. Damon smiled sheepishly, and I was about to put my arms around him when Lacey decided it was time to mess up my night. Shocker.

"I'm cutting in," she said, sliding herself in between Damon and me. She was wearing a very mini black dress, and her hair was all up with little tendrils falling around her face. She looked like she was trying to look eighteen—and failing miserably.

"You have to be kidding me," I said, staring her down.

"Damon doesn't mind," she answered giddily, pulling him away.

I was about to open my mouth to tell Lacey off, because I knew Damon was too polite to do it, when Damon suddenly took Lacey's wrist and removed her hand from his arm. Lacey looked up at him, her mouth dropping open. I was a little stunned too.

"Sorry, Lacey," he said, letting go of her wrist. "I'm all Jessica's tonight."

Lacey's face turned bright red, and I had to bite the inside of my cheek to keep from laughing. She definitely hadn't expected that reaction. Like I said, Damon usually goes with the flow. I felt so incredibly awesome at that moment, I was practically bursting.

Damon slipped his arm around my shoulders and led me to the other side of the living room. "No fights tonight, okay?" he whispered to me as we walked.

"No problem," I answered. But I couldn't resist turning back and sticking my tongue out at Lacey, who narrowed her eyes and stalked off.

Damon shook his head, smiling, and I laughed. "Some things never change," he said.

I turned and put my arms around his neck, and we started to move to the music. Hopefully some things never would change.

Blue

I was leaning back against the snack table, shoveling corn chips into my mouth at a frightening speed, when Damon took a break from dancing, came over, and leaned back next to me.

"Hungry?" he asked, eyeing the nearly empty basket that had been overflowing with chips ten minutes earlier.

"Funny," I said, swallowing my last mouthful. I tried to glance away from the dance floor before he saw what—or who—I was staring at, but it was too late.

"Why don't you just go over there?" Damon asked, nodding in the direction of Elizabeth and Salvador, who hadn't stopped laughing and talking since the moment they'd walked in from the kitchen fifteen minutes ago.

This was so not like me. I don't think I'd ever spent a party wallowing in self-pity. Even at my worst moments I'd always been able to dance and run around and get myself out of my depression. But not this time. Sure, I was glad everyone was friends again. I was glad Elizabeth was happy and having fun. It didn't change the fact that I wished she was happy and having fun with me.

"I can't," I told Damon, wiping my greasy, corn-chip-crumb-covered hands on a bright red napkin, balling it up, and launching it at the garbage can someone had intelligently placed in the corner. After everything that happened, what would Salvador and Elizabeth think if I went over there and "cut in"? They'd probably be afraid I was going to make some big scene or something.

"You can," Damon said, slapping me on the back hard enough to get me away from the table.

I glanced over my shoulder at him and took a deep breath. "Fine," I said. "But if anything goes wrong, it's your fault, dude."

"All me," Damon agreed.

One more deep breath and I was on my way across the dance floor. Elizabeth saw me coming and went a little pale. Exactly the reaction I wanted. Not.

"Hey," I said, shoving my hands in my pockets. I looked up at Salvador. "Mind if I . . . ?"

Salvador looked at me for a moment, obviously confused, then he realized what I was asking and smiled. "Please!" he said. "Take her away before I injure her."

I grinned, and Elizabeth let out a little laugh. Salvador was a good guy, I had to admit it. How annoying.

"Are you up for it?" I asked Elizabeth, my heart pounding.

"Sure," she said. Of course, at that exact moment, as Salvador shuffled off and plopped down on a couch to rest his leg, a slow song started. Because the situation wasn't already awkward enough.

After a moment's hesitation I reached out and put my arms around Elizabeth's waist. She put her arms around my neck and we danced, holding each other about a foot away and barely moving. She was so stiff, you could have ironed clothes on her back.

"Listen, Blue," she said, looking down at our feet. "I know you're still mad at me—"

"Don't worry about it," I interrupted. It came out sounding more angry than I wanted it to. "Really," I added with the sincerity I felt. "Please don't worry about it. I'm sorry I was such a jerk . . . so many times."

She relaxed a little and dared a look into my eyes. "I don't blame you," she said with a half smile.

"And I don't blame you for liking Sal," I said with a shrug. "I mean, the guy can't surf to save his life, but . . ." She laughed, and I felt my heart warm. "But really, he's a great guy, and I just . . . I just want you to be happy."

Elizabeth smiled for real and gave me a quick kiss on the cheek. "You're a great guy, Blue Spiccoli," she said.

I blushed fire-engine red. "Man!" I said, laughing. "The guys in Utah have no idea what they're in for!"

Elizabeth

"Thanks for coming over here," I said to Blue as the song came to an end. "I don't know if I would have had the guts to do the same."

Blue sighed, looking guilty. "Don't ever be afraid to talk to me, all right?" he said. He looked at me pleadingly, and at that second I suddenly knew exactly what Blue had looked like as a little kid. Too cute.

"Deal," I said. I pulled away from him and stuck out my hand, and we shook on our new deal right there on the dance floor. Then Blue smiled and pulled me into a big bear hug.

"You're cool, Elizabeth Wakefield," he said.

"I know," I joked. Over his shoulder I saw Salvador hobbling his way over to us as another slow song started up.

Blue and I broke apart, and Blue put one hand on Salvador's shoulder, one hand on mine. "She's all yours, man," he said. Then he turned and walked off, grabbing a carrot stick off a tray as he headed over to Bianca and Larissa. I couldn't wipe the grin off my face. Blue and I were friends again. Could this night get any better?

"Hey," Salvador said, drawing my attention back to him. I looked up into his big black eyes, and he leaned in closer to me. "Remember when I said everyone was going to miss you?" he asked in a deep whisper.

I nodded. His voice was so full of emotion, it made my spine tingle.

"Well, I'm gonna miss you the most," he said, his voice catching slightly.

I blinked up at him, my heart pounding. I just wanted time to stop right there so I could remember this moment forever. The open, caring look on his face would be burned on my memory for all time. There was so much I wanted to say, but I couldn't make myself speak. If I did, I would cry. I knew I would. But I didn't have to say anything. Because at that moment Salvador leaned forward and kissed me, right there in the middle of my living room, with everyone I knew and loved dancing around me.

It was the most perfect moment ever.

When he broke away, we both smiled. Then he took his crutches and leaned them up against the back of the couch, balancing on his good leg. He wrapped his arms around my waist and held me close as we swayed—just slightly—to the music. I didn't think about the move or leaving my home and friends. All I could think about was Salvador's arms around me.

Then the music picked up again, and everyone cheered. Suddenly it seemed like the whole house was bouncing as everyone started to jump and dance around. Jessica and Damon joined us. Then Kristin, Brian, and Blue came over. Then Anna pulled Bethel and Larissa over too. Before I knew it, all of our best friends were jumping up and down in one big cluster, hugging, laughing, and acting like silly little kids.

Everyone was having an amazing time. And at that moment nothing else mattered.

Timeline

8:45 P.M. Mr. Wakefield walks into his house to find the most raging party he's ever seen his kids involved in. He grins when he sees his daughters dancing with their friends, smiling like he hasn't seen them smiling in days. He puts down his bag and makes a bee-line for his wife.

8:46 P.M. Blue watches as Mr. Wakefield kisses Mrs. Wakefield hello, then whispers something in her ear. Mrs. W.'s face lights up brightly, and she nods a silent yes. Blue elbows Bethel to bring it to her attention.

8:46 P.M. Bethel looks at Mrs. Wakefield's beaming face, then leans over and tells Kristin there's something going on. Kristin takes one look at the parentals and agrees, then whispers into Jessica's ear. Jessica grabs Elizabeth and tells her their dad is home. The twins excuse themselves and maneuver across the room to their parents.

8:48 P.M. Anna watches as, seconds after Elizabeth and Jessica greet their dad,

Elizabeth goes off to the den and comes back with Steven. Anna nudges Salvador and asks him what's going on.

8:49 P.M.   Salvador watches as Mr. Wakefield tells the entire Wakefield family something, and they all grin and cheer and hug one another. He knocks Damon with his crutch. After rubbing his arm and shooting Salvador a dirty look, Damon notices the little Wakefield celebration in progress. Elizabeth and Jessica are clutching each other, and Steven has all four limbs wrapped around his dad like he's two years old. Damon looks around at their friends, confused, and their expressions all mirror his. What's going on?

8:51 P.M.   Steven snaps off the CD player, and the whole crowd goes silent. Jessica climbs up onto the coffee table that's pushed against the wall, pulling Elizabeth up with her. "We have an announcement to make," Jessica says, grinning. At the same time she and Elizabeth both shout at the top of their lungs. "We're not moving!!!"

Jessica

As I dragged Bethel, Kristin, and Lila out onto the patio once again, I felt like I was about to burst with happiness. I couldn't stop laughing. It was so hard to believe that just a few days ago I'd been about to burst with anger. Now my parents had made me the happiest person on earth. We weren't moving! Instead of remembering this night forever as bittersweet, I would just remember it as sweet, sweet, sweet!

We sat down on patio chairs and were joined by all of my friends, three or four people crowding onto each lounge chair. Damon and Brian brought out plastic cups of punch and carefully handed them out to everyone. Then Salvador limped through the back door with Elizabeth at his side. She sat down across from me, and if we'd ever looked like mirror images of each other, we definitely did now. We had the same exact stupid, goofy smile on our faces.

"So? What's the deal?" Anna asked when everyone was settled.

"Yeah, what the heck happened back there?" Toby asked, squeezing in between Larissa and Bethel.

"My dad just came home from work and told us he'd changed his mind," I explained, shrugging giddily. "He said the more he thought about it and talked it over with my mom, the more they both realized that the new job wasn't worth taking all of us away from our friends and our home."

"Plus his boss offered him a huge raise if he'd stay," Elizabeth added in a matter-of-fact voice. Everyone laughed, and Salvador slipped his arm around her shoulders. It didn't even bother me at that moment that my sister was falling for a dweeb. At least he was a nice dweeb, and now she'd get to be with him just like I was going to get to be with Damon!

"I think he would have decided to stay, money or no money," I said, preferring to take the sentimental train of thought. "There are too many memories here." Elizabeth and I gazed up at our house—the window of the room we used to share, the tree she'd fallen out of in second grade, breaking her arm in two places, the pool where we swam on every single Christmas Eve.

Then Elizabeth looked around at all our friends. "There would have been too many good-byes," she said, getting all misty-eyed.

"Aw!" Bethel, Kristin, and Anna all teased in unison. Everyone cracked up again.

"So I guess you're stuck with us!" I said, grinning from ear to ear.

Salvador sighed and rolled his eyes, letting out an exasperated snort. "Great," he said sarcastically.

"Very funny," Elizabeth said, nudging him with her leg.

Damon cleared his throat and stood, holding up his glass of punch. "I guess I'd . . . uh . . . like to propose a toast," he said, and cleared his throat again. He wasn't much for speaking in public, so I was flattered he was even trying.

"To Elizabeth and Jessica," he said.

"And to their parents," Kristin added.

"And to the guy who gave your dad a raise," Salvador put in.

We all laughed.

"And to never-ending friendships," Elizabeth added, snaking her free hand through the crook in Blue's arm.

"And to good times that will never end," I said.

We all just paused and looked at one another for a moment, taking it all in.

"So drink up!" Larissa finally shouted.

We all cheered and downed our glasses. Damon leaned over and kissed me, and I saw

Jessica

Brian kiss Kristin and Salvador kiss Elizabeth and Toby kiss Anna. Suddenly it felt like New Year's Eve. After glancing around at all the couples, Blue grabbed Ronald and dipped him back, fake kissing him like a madman.

"Now let's dance!" I called out when all the lip smacking was through. Everyone was up in an instant, and we all made our way back to the living room, where the rest of the guests were still grooving. Even my parents were getting down in the middle of the makeshift dance floor. I caught Elizabeth's eye, and we both shook our heads, but I wasn't about to stop them. Who cared if they were embarrassing? They were happy!

Suddenly Damon grabbed me up in a hug and spun me around. I screeched but then just started laughing as the whole room, filled with friendly faces I'd be seeing for a long, long time, twirled around me.

There had never been a more perfect party, a more perfect night, a more perfect moment. When he put me down, I hugged my sister tight. Now that we were staying in Sweet Valley, it really did seem like the good times were never going to end.

Check out the **all-new**....

Sweet Valley Web site—

www.sweetvalley.com

New Features

Cool Prizes

The **ONLY** official Web site!

Hot Links

And much more!

BFYR 217